ORIGINAL WORLDS

BOOK TWO

NIGEL RUDDIN

aldon

For Mylo & Casimir

Cover & illustrations: Peter Morey
Page design: Michael Morey

CONTENTS

FOREWORD 5

MUSTIQUE THE BITER 7

BUZZ: AN EXCITING ADVENTURE 16

ARACHNID PHOBIA 25

JUMBLY THING 37

SLUGGISH BEHAVIOUR 51

DRAGON FIRE 62

LIGHTENING 75

BOAR CONSTRICTOR 95

BUBBLES AND ATMOSPHERE 107

AN IRISH GHOST STORY 121

THE SNEEZE 123

HAPPINESS 124

SINISTER 125

HIS RAGE 126

FOREWORD

Planet Earth has an interesting history, there are many vagaries in its existence. The major question must be are we alone out there or are there other sentient beings. There are millions of star systems in our galaxy which probably are the home worlds of many different species. Our belief must be that life exists in many different forms spread across the galaxy. Strange and exotic creatures harbouring immense powers may exist in the far-flung star systems across our galaxy. Then the problem will be when a mile-long spaceship descends on planet Earth and all our puny weapons are useless against this alien intruder. The startling fact is that an alien invasion is a distinct possibility. These tales of the inhabitants of these far-flung planets, illustrate that planet Earth is a tiny speck on the vast spectrum of the universe.

MUSTIQUE THE BITER

A billion light years from a planet known as Earth lived a creature that spread disease and death. Many years ago, the ancestor of this creature had originated a new disease that became known as the black death or the bubonic plague. It was described as a pestilence that was passed on by flees to rodents. This creature whom we will name Biter, was the direct link to the scourge known as the black death. His atoms had been transported vast distances across space through light refraction.

The Biter was huge by Earth's measurements and was almost ten feet in length. Biter didn't feel anything was amiss with his development, but he had nothing to compare himself with. He felt quite elegant in the air as he drifted through the bright red clouds. However, he hadn't quite mastered the landing process and frequently crashed into the ground in a heap. Somehow, he knew that he was a mosquito. He also knew that there were thousands of his species that were spread throughout the star systems of the universe. He also knew that one of his family was the anopheline. Mosquitos were responsible for spreading malaria. Having practiced his gliding skills for the umpteenth time, he perfected the perfect descent and glided perfectly onto the slightly uneven slope. Almost immediately he felt that something had invaded his sub-conscience. Sitting on a large mound surveying him was an enormous bird.

"I feel that I should eat you except for the fact you look totally indigestible," said the large bird.

"You do have a point whatever you are. By the way, my name is Raven said the extremely large bird.

"Nice to make your acquaintance. I am called Biter" he replied.

"That is a very strange name. Why are you called Biter?" demanded the Raven.

"Well, I suppose that it has something to do with my history, unfortunately. My species used to inject a virulent substance that replaced the healthy part of the human body" replied Biter.

"Now I am really confused. What is a human body?" queried Raven.

"That is an entirely different story, but I will endeavour to precis it where possible. Many thousands of years ago, there was a planet known as Earth.. Their scientists were incredibly advanced and could perform wonderful feats that would be far above your imagination. Their scientists warned humanity on numerous occasions about something that was known as global warming. However, humanity seemed to scoff at the risk and carried on making their planet completely inhabitable by poisoning their atmosphere," said Biter.

"Well, what an extraordinary story are you sure that it isn't fabricated?" queried Raven.

"There is absolutely no reason to believe that I keep implying that it is a story, but this is no story but an absolute fact. The atoms that I was endowed with have relayed this message a million times. It is built into my inner being," said Biter.

"This is getting stranger and stranger by the second what do you mean by your inner being?" questioned Raven.

"There again it is quite difficult to explain. It is some kind of predictive memory that correlates to something that occurred in the past," said Biter.

"I have to tell you that our conversations seem to be becoming weirder and weirder, maybe we should discuss something else?" pleaded Raven.

"Yeah, well you have a point, but I have discovered that my distant memories do have a significant impact on the future" replied Biter.

The next instant their conversation was rudely interrupted by a haze of minute insects that seemed intent on attacking them. However, they were no match for the disgruntled duo who fended them off with swipes from their huge wings. Raven came up with a novel comment.

"Pesky varmints" he called them. Biter hadn't a clue of what he meant but smiled knowingly. Raven then inquired if Biter was able to fly as he had enormous wings. Biter's immediate response was to soar up into the sky and dive-bomb Raven, who had to throw himself madly to one side to avoid a collision.

"Ok, I acknowledge that you are master of the air, now can you please slow down" begged Raven.

Biter slowed down immediately to comply with Raven's request. Then in front of them, the sky darkened considerably as if to warn of an impending disaster. Then the thunderheads rose dramatically to herald the arrival of the approaching storm. Sheet lightning blazed across the sky to be followed by an ominous rumble. Then the sluice gates of the heavens opened, and a deluge was released upon them. Torrents of yellow sulphurous water swept down onto them. Both Raven and Biter sored into the air out of harm's way. The downpour was so horrendous that they were both terribly fatigued when they made it out of the eye of the storm.

"Well, I didn't enjoy that as the lightest, the rain and the wind certainly buffeted us to extremes," said Raven. Biter nodded in agreement but remained silent. Both were sitting on a small hillock which allowed the water to flow downhill between them.

"What is your plan now?" inquired Raven. It was a complete shock, but Biter realized that somehow Raven had adopted him as the leader. However, the matter was entirely taken out of his hands as swooping toward them was one of the largest nastiest monsters that they had ever seen.

"Take evasive action!" was Biter's immediate response. Both flew their separate ways and started to zigzag to confuse the incoming hostile. The vast creature seemed to be bemused by this concerted action.

Eventually, the creature shouted out as if he refused to take part in the game.

"Stop it, immediately, you are making me dizzy with all this jitter-bugging action".

"Oh, you poor creature we have no desire whatsoever to give you a headache, but have you looked in the mirror recently, you are probably one of the most horrible and grotesque creatures we have ever encountered. What exactly are you?" demanded Biter.

"Yeah, I know that I am quite original in appearance but that is because there is only one of me. I am a Slobber-stink. However, you can call me Roger" replied the creature.

"Well, at least we know who you are and what you are. I suppose that's a start," said Raven.

"Yes well, I have no intention of sitting around here all day, let's fly" said Biter.

The trio took off in unison, the only problem being that Roger was extremely ungainly and ponderous. Both Raven and Biter had to keep circling back to make sure that Roger was still with them. They flew toward the setting sun and suddenly the lights turned off and they were in pitch black. It was so stygian that they were unable to continue their journey and decided to camp for the night. Dawn broke with a crash which was quite literal as a huge tree had fallen not too far from where they had camped. They took to the skies and were soon on their way. In the distance, they could see huge forests that seemed to stretch on forever. Strange barking noises rose from the ground and packs of hungry wolves passed underneath them. Eventually, Biter, who seemed to have made himself supreme commander, called a halt.

"We seem to be flying vast distances with no plan for our destination. I suggest that we come up with a plan that meets all our needs" suggested Biter.

"The major problem that we have is that we are unsure of the topography of the land, and it is quite difficult to plan any route although we do have the advantage of having an aerial view," said Raven.

Biter, who by then had promoted himself to the commander-in-chief, nodded in agreement at the difficulty they faced in topography. They continued to fly onwards until rising above them was a massive mountain trio that was completely shattered from their arduous journey. They descended into a plateau that was guarded by massive pines and settled down for the night.

They woke to the sound of a cacophony of birds that were enjoying the early morning dawn. There was a hazy mist hanging over the plateau that gave a bleary aspect to their surroundings. As far as nourishment was concerned, they had survived on huge quantities of bongo nuts that were ultra-satisfying and packed full of vitamins.

They took off from the plateau full of high spirits and nuts. The sky was incredibly clear, and they were able to see for miles ahead. A large flock of birds was heading directly for them.

"There must be at least a couple of hundred of them, they are known as suicide birds and will have no compunction in attacking larger birds and unfortunately, we fall, into that category. But at least we have a few minutes before they arrive" said Raven,

"Oh, I shouldn't worry about them. I have a little trick that will simply blow their minds," said Roger.

Having said this, he seemed to enter a mode of extreme concentration. Then something extraordinary started happening to him. He started to grow at a fantastic rate. He expanded and carried on growing until he was as large as a small mountain. Both Raven and Biter hastily removed themselves from his immediate vicinity to allow him room for his rapid expansion. Eventually, he managed to curtail his growth and hung in space like a small planet. In the meantime, the flock of suicide birds that had been approaching quite swiftly veered off in a completely different direction. Having ascertained that the suicide birds had now departed, Roger hung in space for a little while longer, and he unleashed a hurricane on his immediate surroundings.

"Well done. That was an extraordinary piece of timing and you certainly put the suicide birds to flight," said Biter.

"Yeah, I played my part to perfection, and I suppose that it makes me one of the team," said Roger.

"You have always been part of the team as you so delightfully phrase it. As there are only three of us it is not exactly a huge deal," said Biter.

"It is for me. I have always felt to be the runt of the litter, useless and nobody wants me" replied Roger.

"I know exactly how you feel, there is nothing worse than feeling like you are one of life's rejects," said Raven.

"Do you know we may be a crack team, but we are a vibrant team, and we are going to exploit our worst nightmares!" said Biter.

The trio took off in unison, the only problem being that Roger was extremely ungainly and ponderous. Both Raven and Biter kept circling back to make sure that Roger was still with them. They flew towards the setting sun and suddenly the lights turned off and they were in pitch black. It was so stygian that they were unable to continue their journey and decided to camp for the night. Dawn broke with a crash, which was quite literal as a huge tree had fallen not far from where they had camped. They took to the skies and were soon on their way. In the far distance, they could see huge forests that seemed to stretch on forever. Strange barking noises rose from the ground and packs of hungry wolves passed underneath them. Eventually, Biter, who had made himself supreme commander called a halt.

"We seemed to be flying vast distances, without any plan for our destination. I suggest that we come up with a final plan that meets all our needs" suggested Biter.

"The major problem that we have is that we are totally unsure of the topography of the land, and it is quite difficult to plan any route, although we do have the advantage of an aerial view," said Raven.

Biter who by then had promoted himself to commander in chief nodded in agreement at the difficulty they were facing in their journey. They continued to fly onwards until rising above them was a massive mountain range. The trio was completely shattered by their arduous journey and descended into a forest guarded by towering pines and settled down for the night. They awoke to the sounds of a cacophony of birds that sang through the forest to celebrate the early morning dawn. There was a mist hanging over the plateau that gave a bleary aspect to their surroundings. As far as nourishment was concerned, they survived on huge quantities of bongo nuts that were packed full of vitamins. They took off in high spirits and were full of nuts. The sky ahead of them was incredibly clear and they were able to see into the far distance. A large flock of birds was heading directly for them.

"There must be at least a couple of hundred of them, they are. Known as suicide birds and have no fear of attacking larger birds, unfortunately, we fall into that category but at least we have a couple of minutes before they arrive," said Raven.

"Oh, I shouldn't worry about them I have a trick that will simply blow their minds," said Roger.

Having said that, he seemed to enter a mode of extreme concentration. Then something extraordinary started happening. He started to grow at a fantastic rate. He expanded and carried on growing until he was as large as a small mountain. Both Raven and Biter hastily removed themselves from his immediate vicinity to allow him room for his rapid expansion. Eventually, he managed to curtail his growth and hung in space like a small planet In the meantime the suicide birds that had approached so rapidly had veered off in numerous different directions. Then having ascertained that the suicide birds had now departed. Roger. hung in space for a while longer and then released a hurricane on his immediate surroundings, this had been caused by the rapid deflation of his created world.

"Well done, that was an extraordinary piece of timing and you certainly put those suicide birds to flight," said Biter.

"Yeah, I played. my part to perfection and I suppose that makes me one of the team now," said Roger.

"You have always been part of the team as you so delightfully phrase it and as there are only three of us it is no big deal," said Biter.

"It is for me I have always felt myself to be the runt of the litter, useless and nobody wants me" replied Roger.

"I know exactly how you feel, there is nothing worse than feeling that you are one of life's rejects" responded Raven.

"Do you know we may not be a crack team, but we are a vibrant team, and we are going to exploit our worst nightmare?" said Biter.

"What can be our worst nightmare? questioned Roger.

Then with no warning, the sky above them darkened into an impenetrable mass of seething hostility and lightning zigzagged across the sky. This was closely followed. By a massive clap of thunder as if the planet had collided with its sister planet in another dimension. Then even more perturbing, the planet adopted a spinning motion that threatened to whirl them into hyperspace. Then the spinning motion stopped abruptly, and the planet took on an aspect of peace and tranquillity.

"Well, what was all that about?" questioned a perplexed Roger.

"I think that it is a distinct possibility, that our planet has acquired a new personality and wants to establish itself," said Biter.

That must be one of the most ridiculous ideas that I have ever come across a planet that thinks," laughed Raven.

"Not as absurd as you may think, our planet has become sentient and wishes to control our destiny," said Biter.

Then much to their amazement, a huge red orb appeared in the sky above them and uninvited thoughts entered their minds.

"You are just a few minimalistic entities that have entered my world. True you have progressed significantly to invite my interest. However, you have trespassed in this country which I hold very dear to me,"said the entity.

"Well, I am sure that you understand our position, as we have just been created and are the new kids on the block," said Biter

"Yeah, being omnipotent I comprehend your position entirely and intend to make you rulers of this planet, you will have the power over life and death," said the entity.

"Ok, but there seem to be oodles of inhabitants on this planet are you sure that we will be up to the task?" said Roger.

"Well, if you are not, I will cut your heads off and replace you immediately", said the entity.

The trio were never quite certain if he was certain or not. but it did have the effect that they tried even harder. to accomplish their mission.

IN A STAR SYSTEM A BILLION LIGHT YEARS FROM A PLANET THAT WAS FORMERLY KNOWN AS EARTH. THE PLANET WAS RULED BY A TRIO OF LIKEMINDED CREATURES WHO CARED ABOUT THE INHABITANTS OF THEIR PLANET

BUZZ
AN EXCITING ADVENTURE

He wasn't too certain from where he had arrived but felt that it was a long? distance away. He seemed to be encased in a flexible material that allowed him freedom of movement. He stretched his body to its ultimate limit and then a further thought invaded his mind. what sex are you? perhaps you are a hermaphrodite. This thought confused him or her even further. Decisions had to be made and he decided that he must be a male. Therefore, because he had decided that he was a male he instantly became more decisive. He also discovered that although he seemed to be encased in a malleable material, his mind was able to explore the immediate vicinity. Something banged into his malleable cocoon. His conveyance took the blow and started spinning. Amazingly a feeling of calm and tranquillity seemed to be enshrouding him. His traveling compartment became totally translucent, and he was able to forage far and wide with his vision. He immediately noted that the object that had collided with him and started him spinning, seemed to be roughly the same size as his transporter. Then to his consternation, whatever was hidden in the transporter suddenly sat up. As the transporter, like his own, was translucent He realized that it contained a creature that seemed to be staring at him. He then realized that the fellow traveler may be trying to contact him. Then an astonishing thing happened. This creature, whatever it was, seemed to be co-inhabiting the same conveyance as Spin. From where that ridiculous name popped into his head, he hadn't a clue. Still, for the first time since his creation, he had something to call himself by. In the next instant, something that was incredibly weird happened to Spice. The container traveling-traveling vessel expanded dramatically and both translucent vessels clamped together in a loving embrace. The other creature, whatever it was, lay beside Spice. Then the other creature turned and regarded Spin with a quizzical expression on its face. Spin knew that the other creature had a face when he stared into a mirror image of himself.

"Who are you?" He heard himself saying.

"I am your alter ego" replied the being.

"What exactly do you mean?" Demanded Spice

"I am a doppelganger of yourself, but I am possibly in another dimension" fired back the quick reply.

"Then I am even more confused, what exactly is a doppelganger and how are we communicating through our minds?" Requested Spice.

"Yeah, it's extremely complicated but your first question should have been. What is another dimension?"Replied the being.

"Very Well, what is another dimension?" queried Spice.

The creature alongside him turned its head and communicated in his mind.

"Another dimension is exceedingly difficult to explain. It is in effect a parallel universe where everything could be replicated. On the other hand, it may not be anything like that" communicated the creature.

"Well, it seems to me that you haven't an inkling about our existence and why we have been created"complained Spice.

"Anyway, what is Your name? demanded Spice"

The creature became very hesitant, and Spice could ascertain had become quite crestfallen.

"I haven't got a name I am nobody" came back the reply.

"Well, you have a strange name, but I will call you nobody"stated Spice.

Then much to Spin's alarm through the translucent side of the craft he realized that his vessel was descending quite rapidly to a distant planet. Then

The craft that had been their prison, was still rapidly descending. Through their translucent aperture Spin observed a huge planet that seemed to be their obvious destination. The craft entered some kind of gravity shield that slowed down its descent and they glided down and came to a gentle stop.

Nobody was staring at Spice with a transfixed look of amazement spreading across his features. Spin stretched himself and rose to his feet.

"Where are you going?" demanded an alarmed Nobody.

"I am venturing out to conduct a scientific reconnaissance to find the lie of the land" replied Spice.

Spice then forced his way out of the container and climbed out on the ground. He then heard a thump behind him and realized that Nobody had followed his example. The ground seemed to be very uneven and was covered in a mystical sheen. The planet was bathed in light, from what appeared to be a glowing mass in the sky.

"Whatever is up there is extremely hot"moaned Spice.

"Well, for me it's a perfect ambient temperature,"said Nobody.

"Do you know I had a feeling that you would disagree with me in a most disagreeable way" grumbled Spice.

Both had emerged from their prison and were standing by the side of their craft when an object flashed over their heads and plummeted down on a small hillock and exploded. Fragments of the mystical green material rained down on them. A huge chunk of the strange material landed on Nobody and drove him down to his knees.

"Are you all right"? Questioned a worried Spice.

"Well, that is incredible. I didn't know you cared"replied a beaming Nobody..

"Yeah, for all I know we are the only identical creatures that exist from where we came from"Spice replied.

"Then perhaps we should perambulate a little more and discover the lie of the land" suggested Nobody.

"Now that is a sensible suggestion, we probably should investigate the meteorite hit on the small hillock and survey the damage that it has caused" replied Spice.

Both Nobody and Spin toiled up the hill until they reached the summit. The view was spectacular. The vista stretched into the far distance encompassing a massive volcano that was belching out massive streams of fire and smoke.

"Well, at least we know where that exploding rock came from. It seems to be getting even more irate with its predicament as time goes by," said Spice.

"Yeah, it is a massive volcano, the way, that rock flew by it was obviously flexing its muscles,"said Nobody.

"Very descriptive and quite poetic, our conversations are obviously doing you a power of good" replied Spice.

"I am not sure whether I should take this as a scolding or a compliment," said a confused Nobody.

"Well, whatever you decide.to do, I suggest that we get out of the way of that enormous creature that is striding towards us," said Spice

The creature striding towards them was truly gargantuan. He was over ten feet tall and had an expression on his face as if he had a nasty smell under his nose. However, Spice was an incredibly fast mover and didn't agree to have any interruption to his conversation with Nobody. He pranced around the giant whose facial expression began to take on an aura of befuddlement. Spice's dance of exuberance made a mockery of the ponderance of the giant, who was also incredibly clumsy. Eventually, the bemused giant collapsed with a thunderous crash. Then inexplicably he lay on his back and howled with laughter. The permanent smell that had hung under his nostrils had completely disappeared to be replaced by a beatific smile of contentment.

"You know whomever you are? Yes, I am sure that you both know each other. I found your antics most amusing, especially the spinning one," said the giant."By the way, I am called Stupid," said the giant.

"Well, we all have to bear the names that we are saddled with extreme fortitude" retorted Spice.

"However, then in your case, your name seems to be quite applicable"continued Spice.

"Thank you" replied Stupid. not comprehending in the slightest, the fool, he was making of himself.

"My suggestion would be that we trudge up the hill in the direction of the volcano and make our plans for our next moves on the way up," said Spice.

"I totally concur, whatever that means," said Stupid.

The three of them trudged up the hill in the direction of the volcano, which seemed to be suffering from violent indigestion. Huge fireballs were hurled into the sky and intense rumblings were emitted from the crater. The sky in front of the ascending climbers had now turned into a forbidding shade of darkness. Lightening flashed and zigzagged out of the gigantic volcano, enhancing a feeling of impending doom. A large boulder bounded down the hill toward them. Stupid swatted it to one side as if it was irrelevant.

There were still quite a few miles to go until they reached the summit of the volcano. However, they had no intention of spending the night in such a hostile environment, so they forged onwards. If anything, the volcano's Indigestion was becoming worse most of the volcano seemed to be in a constant state of vibration. They had just climbed up an escarpment and rounded a corner when they were faced by a huge lizard. It stared at them balefully. The trio received a message at the same time.

"I must say that the three of you look completely inedible and with this in mind, I will be forced to exterminate you,"said the sneering lizard.

"Well, you are an extremely large animal, but I am of equal size, so how do you propose to eliminate us?""Questioned Stupid.

"You must be entirely stupid to think that I will not find a way to exterminate you," said the lizard.

"Yes, I am" came back the instant reply.

"Yes, I am what? Queried the lizard.

"Yes, I am Stupid in its entirety" replied Stupid.

"In that case because of your stupidity, I deem it necessary to act as your guide. The paths around here are extremely dangerous, and I wouldn't want you falling into the volcano," said the lizard.

"Well, this is a change of heart, the manner in which you were postering led me to believe that you were one of the bad guys," said Spice.

The four of them started on their journey, the lizard leading the way. The incline became steeper and more precarious as they climbed ever upwards. A stream of magma flowed down the hill, and then at the last minute, it diverted the course. They were still a couple of miles from the summit of the volcano, but the heat was becoming more intense the further up they ascended.

They approached the last climb up to the volcano gingerly. It was still belching forth innumerable foul-smelling gasses and the occasional rock, projectile.

Eventually, they reached the summit of the volcano. Staring down into the incandescent void, they encountered a million different rainbows that constantly changing colours.

"What is that dreadful smell that is pervading our nostrils?" Demanded Nobody.

"Do you really expect an answer to that? As you are that vacant creature that doesn't exist Nobody said Spice.

Just as Spice finished his comment, a huge figure started to emerge from the volcano. It was covered in green scales and carried a large trident in its left hand.

"Let me out I am totally stuck, and my bottom is on fire" moaned the creature.

"Well for a ten-thousand-foot monstrosity, you have such an evil aspect, I am tempted to leave you there," said Spice.

"You do know that the complete scenario is a figment of your imagination?" Questioned the lizard.

He then continued."You have just ingested a vast amount of nitrous oxide, which is more commonly known as laughing gas. Your imagination probably took you on a fascinating journey and no doubt you encountered some very interesting people"continued the lizard.

"Well, as far as I am concerned this whole area around the volcano smells terrible"complained Spin.

"That is because you are constantly inhaling vast quantities of hydrogen sulphide, smells of rotten eggs & sometimes known as laughing gas"commented Nobody.

"Then it appears that we have a chemical genius in our midst" quipped Spin.

"Yes, I don't think that is very fair, I have no wish to become distinguished in any way I would like to retain my identity as a nobody" replied Nobody.

"Unfortunately, and it may just be semantics, but you have added A, which could infer that it is a definite article, and, in that case, you can't possibly be a nobody," said Spin.

"Well, here are all three of us peering into the crater of a volcano what do we do from here?" said the lizard.

"For us, that is incredibly easy, chimed in both Spice & and Nobody. We will combine"

Then before the incredulous gaze of the lizard, an amazing transformation took place. Both Spin and Nobody seemed to flow into other's bodies. This appeared to be a perfect unification" exclaimed both.

"Then who are we in our new doppelganger body?" They questioned.

"Well, it's difficult to explain but you are me and I am you. Our intelligence will thrive, and our success will know no limits"chimed the duo.

"That is the most absurd thing that I have ever heard. You whomever you are? are claiming that you have been gifted with superpowers. Therefore, if I were to jump into this volcanic crater you would immediately spirit me out," said the lizard.

"Yes, that service would be available to you" chimed the duo.

The izard thought for a moment, before girding his loins, then he thought this is an adventure, and jumped. For a moment the lizard thought that he had made a stupid mistake as the walls of the crater flashed past him. Then he slowed down dramatically, which was to his detriment as the seething caldron below him started to roast him. Then again everything changed, and a cool breeze started to fan him. The lizard then found himself lying in a field of grass that seemed to stretch on forever under a blue sky. Peering down at him was either Spice or nobody, he couldn't be certain.

"Well, that wasn't so bad, was it?" said the duo.

"For you perhaps not, but I found the occasion the most terrifying experience that I have ever encountered," said a trembling lizard.

"Then, you have probably learned one important thing, trust" replied the duo

"You had the courage to hurl yourself into the crater. This was purely based on the premise of trust continued" the duo.

"Well, you have obviously been gifted with immense powers, how do you intend to use them?" questioned the lizard

"Wisely" came back with a quick reply and without any hesitation.

In a star system, a trillion light years away. A beneficial duopoly RULES The Planet with a SYSTEM OF KINDNESS AND CARE

ORIGINAL WORLDS BOOK TWO

24

ARACHNID PHOBIA

A couple of million years ago there was a violent explosion on a planet that was known as Earth. Unfortunately, the inhabitants of this doomed planet didn't heed the frequent advice of their scientists about global warming from greenhouse gases. This resulted in temperatures soaring to an unprecedented level. Sea levels rose dramatically due to the melting ice caps, and vast tracks of land became flooded because of the warming. The land became increasingly scarce, and nations took up arms against each other sometimes to defend themselves against invaders and sometimes being the invaders. Humankind found itself in a dreadful situation as many of them possessed huge stockpiles of nuclear weapons Eventually because of the preponderance of weapons the larger nations succeeded in wiping each other out. Hence the explosion that exterminated all of humanity. However, Spin wasn't aware of his extraordinary escape from planet Earth. Yet something else he was unaware of was that whilst he was in his travel mode he was in suspended animation. Spin, this was the name that he called himself although he didn't know why, for thousands of years, he travelled to an unknown destiny without knowing his destination. Occasionally, he would wake up for an instant and reflect on his innermost thoughts, he decided that he didn't like himself. furthermore, he decided that he detested himself, without understanding why. Spin. voyaged on passing through star systems containing vast belts of radioactivity. Spin didn't realize what was happening to him as he passed through yet another field of radioactivity. He was infusing within. himself an enormous growth potential that propagated his atoms with an explosive force and continued to multiply. Spin had transformed from a small spider-like creature to a gigantic behemoth of frightening stature. However, inside, the frightening aspect of Spin resided the tiny, diminutive creature that had set out from planet Earth thousands of years before. Then suddenly, they had arrived at a huge gas giant that was spouting out vast quantities of sulphur and noxious gases. However, this planet contained no fears for Spin as he thought that the planet appeared quite normal.

"Well, you are a bizarre-looking creature. I don't know where you are from or where you are going.? But, nevertheless, I bid you welcome" said a resonating voice from the planet.

"Yeah, I have been voyaging over vast distances and I am not sure where I am going or if indeed, I have got there:". replied Spin.

"Yes, I can honestly say that you are probably one of the most well-travelled beings in all the universe by the way my name is Joe, and we are situated on the planet Grind,"said Joe.

"Well, thank you for all the information, but I am still rather confused, are you some kind of god?" questioned Spin.

"That is a wrong supposition, I am the complete planet that totally relies on me. Then having said that. I probably can perform certain miraculous acts that may be construed to be godlike powers," said Joe.

"Ok, we seem to be getting somewhere. However, my next question must be is there any life on planet Grind?" demanded Spin.

"Yes, there is a very primitive form of something, and I am not sure what it is?" replied Joe.

"Well, something as primitive as your description doesn't sound too dangerous to me," said Spin.

"Then, I have a proposition to put to you. Would you like to settle on my planet? As the predominant life form queried Joe.

"Well, I am certainly grateful for the offer, and I would have to think about it. The problem is that there is only one of me" replied Spin.

"That is where you are so wrong. and probably because you passed through so many areas of radioactivity that your atoms exploded and granted you the gargantuan figure that you are today,"said Joe.

Then without further ado, Joe glazed over a huge section of the planet and turned it toward Spin. Then for the first time in his epic journey, Spin was able to see the gargantuan figure that he had turned into.

"Don't worry about the trillion atoms. that make up your body I should be able to split them up into smaller quantities," said Joe.

"Do you know what I have learned about you in an exceedingly? short time is that you have definitely assumed godlike powers. For another example you turned planet Grind completely around enabling me to have a mirror image of myself." said Spin.

Ok I must admit that I have been showing off slightly but only with your best interests at heart," said Joe

Over the next few weeks, incredible things happened to Spin. He didn't notice it at first but then realized that he was shrinking. Joe then explained to him that the reason for the shrinkage was that he had split the atoms that had comprised his body into far smaller quantities and then reassured him by saying that he was still a giant being over seven feet tall.

"There is one other thing that I have arranged for you, that I am sure will enhance your lifestyle," said Joe.

"Yeah, it sounds interesting, but what are you talking about?" replied Spin.

"How would you feel, about having a female as your life partner?" Questioned Joe.

"Fine, but what is a female?" inquired Spin.

"OK, I can envisage that we may have a problem. However, I suggest that our best option must be to leave everything to me, and I will sort out the problem. However, I am not an embryologist, but it should be fine," said Joe.

Poised on the end of Spin's tongue was a pertinent question what is an embryologist? However, on reflection, he decided to remain silent, and nothing emerged.

Joe, on the other hand, had been very industrious in searching for a lifetime partner for Spin. Eventually, by extraordinary manipulation, he discovered the ideal lifetime partner for Spin. As Spin had disappeared for a short time, Joe decided to wait for his return. In the meantime, he had dreamed up a name for Spin's partner would name her Lilly. When Spin returned in his usual rumbustious way by hurling himself through the door Joe was waiting for him.

"I have an important introduction to make to you and her name is Lilly," said Joe.

Then there was a gigantic flash and a beautiful woman appeared. To describe her as beautiful was a massive understatement she was stunning. So much so that Spin collapsed on the floor with a resounding thump. Her long golden tresses seemed to have an ethereal glow that flickered in the half-light. There was no point in asking Spin for his approval of Lilly as his obvious joy was perfectly obvious.

"What. do, you think of my creation do you like her?" asked Joe.

"Thank you" was Spin's only response.

Lilly as yet hadn't even spoken a word. However, in the world of Spin, she didn't need to as he was still enchanted by her beauty. After a few moments, she turned toward him and spoke.

"I feel as if I have been drifting in a perpetual dream that enveloped me completely and was impossible to break out from and wake up," said Lilly.

Spin's immediate reaction to her voice was that it seemed to flow as a perfect melody that touched his innermost desires. Her long blond hair streamed down her back and flowed in every direction. But the one thing that really transfixed him was her piercing blue eyes that flickered with intense feelings of love and devotion. Whether these feelings were directed in his direction or not, he didn't care. Spin just wanted to be in her company forever and a day.

Joe had picked up the intense feelings that were emanating from Spin almost immediately and realized that he better do something about it to solve the problem.

"Lilly, do you find the humanoid seated alongside you in any way attractive?" queried Joe.

"Yes, I do find Spin incredibly attractive. But having just said that how would I know?" as I have only just been created," said Lilly.

"I do think that you have been quite unfair in asking a lady a dubious question such as that,"said Spin.

"Me thinks that he does try and protect the lady's honour"replied Joe

"Well, we seem to be going. backwoods and forwards without making any progress," said Spin.

"I think that we have made incredible progress under the banner of make love, not war," said Joe.

"Now I have become completely confused about what are love and war," said Spin.

"I know what love is, in my dreams, I have already made its acquaintance. It is peace and tranquillity and celestial choirs," said Lilly.

"That doesn't sound very exciting to me and sounds rather dreary," said Spin.

"Do you know something lover boy, you are not as nearly attractive as you were a few minutes ago," said Lilly.

The comment that Lilly had made brought Spin down with a tremendous bump as he was completely infatuated with the blond-haired goddess

Joe ascertained instantly that Spin had been completely deflated by Lilly's caustic comment and decided that he would defend the being that he considered to be his protégée and therefore he intervened on his behalf.

"You may not have realized the situation that you have placed yourself in Lilly, I created you from absolutely nothing except a few atoms. Amazingly. enough these atoms are derived from the atom mass of Spin's original body and to put it simply without Spin you wouldn't even exist"Joe's voice thundered out.

"You are telling me that without Spin I would still be an atom drifting around with nowhere to go?" asked Lilly

"Yeah, well done, that is exactly what I am inferring," said Joe.

"Well, I am not too sure if I believe you and find it most distasteful that I am a former part of Spin,"said Lilly

"Don't worry I have encountered the same problem as you. How can a glorious creature like you be a former part of me?" inquired Spin

"Well, we all seem to be going around in never-ending circles without advancing in the slightest. The main problem appears to be that you Lilly are totally narcissistic and are infatuated with your own appearance," said Joe.

"That comment is incredibly unfair and please tell me what is so wrong with being fantastically as beautiful as I am?" said Lilly.

"OK, they go say that beauty is in the eye of the beholder, and in your case, you have fallen passionately in love with yourself. There is an ancient story that in some ways reminds me of you, about a beautiful mermaid who was so infatuated with her beauty that she sat on a huge rock by the sea combing her tresses. and viewing herself in a mirror. She was so engrossed with her stunning beauty that she lost all sense of time. The Mermaid carried on surveying her beauty for thousands of years. Until she had aged so much that she turned into stone. The mirror fell out of hand and splintered into small shards of glass. The moral of this story is that beauty doesn't last forever and beware of the ravages of time," said Joe.

"But there is no truth in that story, it is just a banal fairy story passed on through the realms of time," said Lilly

"Who knows if it is true or purely a fabrication and quite frankly who cares?" said Joe.

"I care"replied Lilly

Oh, that is Marvelous. I suppose that you regard yourself as a fairytale princess waiting to be rescued from some terrible fate," said Joe.

"That comment is unfair, and I regard myself as no such thing" retorted Lilly.

"Well, I don't think of myself as a fairytale prince, but I would rescue Lilly at any time should the need arise,"said Spin

"Then I must formally retract my previous comment as I find you a million times more attractive than I did a short time ago," said Lilly.

"You have just proved to me without a shadow of a doubt the fickle nature of women which is as changeable as the non-focused weather system," said Joe.

"Then, you don't like women do you?" demanded Lilly

"Put it like this I am not even certain what I am and could be even female, although certainly feel like a male. For example, I also have yet. another problem am I a god or not? Yes, I do have certain magical powers and can control the weather system. However, I am quite glad that I am not omnipotent as I would be carrying the cares of our planet on my shoulders," said Joe

"Well, I have a serious complaint to make," said Spin.

"OK and what is your complaint?" inquired Joe

"Well as you have taken responsibility for control of our weather system, my complaint is the dreadful weather conditions that we have been forced to endure. This includes not only torrential rain and flooding but violent storms that devastated vast tracks of land and destroyed numerous buildings," complained Spin.

"Yes, I must admit that I did allow the weather to run free without any restrictions, but it was extremely exciting don't you think? said, Joe

"Yeah, it was extremely exciting and scary. However, don't you think that your powers may stretch much further than you originally envisaged?" Questioned Spin.

"For example, you have already stated that you have lived for thousands of years. But you don't even know when you were created. This leads me to my next supposition, perhaps you are immortal and live forever? Continued Spin.

"That is extremely unlikely, a thousand years ago I caught a cold, a humanoid, disease, and felt dreadful for a couple of days but eventually I managed to shake it off,"said Joe.

"That proves absolutely zilch, I suppose that even immortals suffer failure to their health?" replied Spin.

"OK, then how about another superb power that you may possess the power to read minds?" asked Spin.

"Yeah, I can do that although sometimes their mind is so full of rubbish that I leave almost immediately," said Joe.

"I hope that you comprehend that the only reason that I am conducting this inquisition is to prove to you categorically that you are a god. However, thinking about this conundrum I realized that I have never actually seen you in the flesh, which is purely a figure of speech as you probably don't have any flesh," said Spin.

"The next instant there was a blinding flash and a large shimmering figure appeared, which. Frequently disappeared before reappearing again.

"Well at least I was correct about the flesh, and it is so nice to meet you in person," said Spin.

The shimmering figure replied immediately.

"Likewise," it responded

"Well, I must say that proving that you are a god or otherwise, has established a big round zero," said Spin.

"Well, you have tried your utmost endeavours. To prove to me that I am a god and for this I must thank you as your arguments gave me food for thought and perhaps after all this, I am a god," said Joe.

Shortly after that, there was a flash of lightning and a boom of thunder and Joe vanished.

"That was spontaneously dramatic and performed with great energy," said Lilly.

"I agree with that comment and surmise that he may be turning into a bit of a drama queen" replied Spin.

"Well, now that you have aroused the spirit of adventure within me, where do we go from here? Questioned Lilly.

The next instant she was soaring up in the clouds and far above the planet and studying her intently was her companion Spin.

"What is happening to me and how did I get up so far above the planet?" asked Lilly.

"You are just as amazed as I am, I used the power of my mind and almost immediately we were floating above the planet" confirmed Spin.

"That is incredible you are telling me that you imagined something and then it happened immediately. Never mind about Joe assuming godlike powers you seem to be assuming them as well," said Lilly.

Then, amazed. with his newfound power, Spin decided to experiment with the gift. He discovered that just by imagining a fictitious location he would be transported there instantly. His experimentation became wilder and wilder as he also created horrific monsters. Spin then began to wonder if the monsters were real, or purely a figment of his imagination. However, he decided that they were realm when one of the monsters took a slice out of his arm. Then purely by utilizing his imagination, he managed to heal himself instantly.

"Having watched you for quite some time you seem to be increasing your powers exponentially all, the time," said Lilly.

"Yes, it is very strange but somehow I seem to be taking in new knowledge all, the time and my mind feels that it is just about to explode," said Spin.

"A little learning is dangerous. thing drink deep or taste not the Pierian spring. There shallow drafts intoxicate the brain and drinking largely sobers us again" said the booming voice of Joe rang out.

"Great poem, but what is the connection with all that we have been through and the current situation?" demanded Spin

The problem is that you are delving deeply into matters that you don't understand"replied Joe.

"Well, believe it or not, I comprehend far more than I did a few months ago, it is all about imagination"repliedSpin.

That is intriguing I didn't know that, perhaps ibis because I live in a cloud and don't get out much," said Joe.

"Then, that must be your problem. You have been isolated in your cloud for so long that you have lost all conception of communication," said Spin.

"You are possibly correct," said Joe and abruptly disappeared.

"Well, he has managed to flit off again in his usual abrupt manner, he is a complete loner,"said Spin.

"Yeah, he is a strange creature and stuck up there in his cloud must-have bags of time for prolonged contemplation," said Lilly

"Ok. then maybe we should formulate a plan for our future strategy." Suggested Spin.

Well, as you seem supremely confident that you can defeat any enemy that the planet may throw at you, I will take a back seat and marvel at your endeavours," said Lilly.

Yeah, I know what I must sound like a braggard. and an unpleasant big-head but I am feeling on top of the world" replied Spin.

Then both of them flew off as Lilly was enwrapped in Spin's imagination, their flight took them over deserts and vast lakes. Then because of the multiple suns of the planet Grind and falling rain, they witnessed purple rainbows that kept flickering and disappearing. Spin sensed that Lilly was probably tiring although all the action was taking part in Spin's imagination. They then flew down to rest for the night and camped in the shadow of a gigantic Obenga tree. When Lilly woke up the next morning, she smelt a delicious. smell that was arising from the fire that he had built

"Good morning it sounded like you slept very well after your arduous day. Our breakfast consists of meadow dewdrops and yellow fungi, this is garnished with a liberal sprinkling of rainbow eggs" said Spin.

"That sounds absolutely delicious," said Lilly

Then having had their breakfast they flew up into the sky again and continued onwards with their journey. The landscape kept changing as they swept over impenetrable jungles and emerald-green lakes. They flew on again supported aloft by Spin's imagination. For an instant, a negative thought invaded his mind."How was it possible that his imagination kept them aloft and flying?"However, he managed to reject the idea immediately as he had a vision of both of them falling out of the sky and being pulverized on the rocks below. They then seemed to be locked into following the course of a river that seemed to flow on for eternity. Then after the thirst-quenching river, they emerged into a sun-blasted desert where nothing moved, and life was short. After the desert Spin made his customary signal and they both flew down.

"Well, that was both educational and exciting and after that huge breakfast I needed a great deal of exercise," said Lilly

"Yeah, but we can't loiter around all day, so we better get moving," said Spin

"Pray, tell me what the hurry is and where are we going?" said Lilly.

"I really haven't a clue where we are going but am sure that we will find out when we get there?" was Spin's response.

Then without further delay, they were on their way and resumed their journey. However, unlike the early part of their journey, the weather conditions were worsening all the time, and ominous black clouds loomed up on the far horizon. Then the gale-force winds hit them with a devastating force and even though Spin's imagination held both of them steady to wait for the storm blowing itself out. Then. Just when the tempest was reaching its crescendo it stopped. and they were bathed in sunlight.

"You didn't heed my warning. I advised you to be careful and you have brought the wrath of the down on your heads," said Joe.

"What utter bunkum, you are the guy who is responsible for controlling the weather and you haven't done a very good job," said Spin

"OK I admit that I took my eye off the job for a second and chaos took over" replied Joe

That is a lame excuse your job is to make sure that the weather functions normally twenty-four-seven," said Spin.

On planet Grind, a planet situated a trillion light-years from the remains of a planet formerly known as Earth. This was a planet entirely different from any of the other planets that you may have visited on your voyages of discovery. This was a planet ruled by imagination as Spin discovered when he visited for the first time. Wars and corruption were consigned to the dustbin of eternal waste and left to drown in their putrification. If you are extremely fortunate may be able to venture, there in your imagination.

JUMBLY THING

He didn't know what he was and appeared to be just a jumble of atoms. However, he had ascertained that he existed. His brain seemed to be whirling around as if it was searching for the truth. whatever that may be.

"What sex are you?" his brain questioned.

"Haven't a clue" was his immediate response.

"Well, at least we seemed to have arrived wherever we were going?" replied his brain.

There was a shuddering deceleration and his or Her's craft came to an abrupt halt. He seemed to be encased in a hard material that contained all his life force. He pushed with all his strength against it, and it flew open with a clatter. Instantly he was exposed to the furious elements of the planet. Except for him, as he exited from the pod, they were not. The area that he emerged into was simply stunning. Exotic, brightly coloured fruit hung from enormous vines that festooned the area. Beyond those tranquil waters lapped on the shores of a sandy beach. His next problem was naming one. He had decided that he was a male which would make him more decisive. He knew nothing of male names and decided to invent one for his own personal use. He asked his brain if he had any ideas for his naming ceremony.

"Yes, I have" came back the quick repost.

"On reflection, because of your endeavours shall name you Action," said the brain.

Action was pleased with his new soubriquet and was determined to live up to his name. He ambled out nonchalantly onto a stretch of pristine sand. Clear blue waters lapped around his feet as he forged through the waters. Something was advising him that the ultimate way to progress was to adopt something called swimming. He threw himself into the water with a mighty splash and cleaved the waters with prodigious strokes. He then realized that swimming alongside him was a striking image of himself. This is absolutely crazy he told himself. I am racing against a mirror image of myself and can never win. However, on the other hand, I can never lose. So, he ploughed gainfully onwards until something warned him to slow down. Perhaps it was sensible advice received from his brain.

Then for the first time in his short existence, he thought

"What the hell I am enjoying this" and drove himself onwards. A numbing sensation then entered his head forcing him to slow down.

"You are behaving in an imbecilic manner; I have found it quite difficult to control your aggressive instincts" complained the brain.

"Well, you did christen me Action, he replied.

"That is very true, but unfortunately you seem to have taken it to extremes" retorted the brain.

Action decided that his conversations seemed to be going round in circles without achieving anything and so he decided to divest himself of the ponderous brain which had been inhibiting him. He had already discovered that he had an affinity with water which enabled him to swim. Perhaps he could master another talent that would grant him yet another method of progress. Just then a vast something or other flew over his head. Yes, I could do that the power of flight should be well within my parameters. Unfortunately, however hard he concentrated on achieving his goal, his feet stayed firmly rooted to the ground.

"You are not doing very well, are you?" a sneering voice had entered his head.

"Go away I don't need you anymore and stop stalking me," said Action.

"That is where you are so wrong, you need me as your personal adviser otherwise you will blunder from pillar to post. What is your problem?" Queried the brain.

"Well, I seem to have an enormous problem, but I suppose that it is better to have two brains concentrating on something than one," said Action.

"Yes, well thought out but we still have a problem I am your brain and there is only one of me but tell me your problem and perhaps we can solve it," said the brain.

"I am not certain if you observed it, but a huge creature passed overhead, and I believe that it is called flying, and I would like to emulate that. I concentrated very intensely but was unable to gain any ascension whatever," said Action.

However, as much as they concentrated on trying to solve the power of flight, they were unable to do so. Action was concentrating so hard that his head started to pulsate with the effort. He had envisaged that he was rising above the ground, but it was to no consequence, and he remained earthbound.

"Well, this seems to be a huge planet that we have landed on, it seems to go on forever," said the brain.

"Yeah, on our way to get here, we passed over vast expanses of ocean and forests, but we were moving so fast that it was exceedingly difficult to take in" stated Action.

"Then it seems to me that we should not procrastinate but investigate," said the brain.

Immediately, Action exploded into overdrive and plunged into the pristine clear waters of the sea. It was a joyful experience as he ploughed onwards through the tranquil waters. Who needs to have an avian mentality? When I can literally fly through these waters. Action then received an urgent warning from the ever-watchful brain.

"Slow down, there is something of monstrous proportions in the waters ahead of you" warned the brain.

Instantly Action slowed down to an elegant pace. As he approached the creature, he began to realize just how vast it was. The most amazing thing about the whole affair was that the creature seemed to be alive. A huge red eye in the creature's head transfixed him as he approached the behemoth. Then Action felt the creature delve into the furthest recesses of his innermost being.

"Well, I must say what a very interesting sentient jumble of atoms you are. I am not certain what kind of creature you are, but you have travelled millions of light-years across the galaxy. I shall call you jumbly thingy

Then Redeye began to glow mischievously.

"You are an interesting creation, and I shall follow your progress with trepidation not knowing how you will evolve," said Redeye.

Then the massive creature dived beneath the waves and in doing so opened a vortex that spun Action in a whirlpool at a frantic rate. Eventually, Action broke free from the clutches of the descending Redeye and exploded into the ocean. He rose to the surface coughing and spluttering.

"Well, that was an interesting confrontation, and I must confirm that the Redeye seemed to have the upper hand" stated the brain.

"Yeah, I wondered when you would pop up again to deliver one of your caustic comments" replied Action.

Action was quite exhausted from his exertions and decided to take it easy. However, he still felt that the brain was still spying on him. He had discovered one thing about himself and that was that he had an innate love of swimming. He launched himself on the surface of the ocean and swam with a powerful crawl. So fast was his speed that he devoured vast tracks of the ocean without realizing it. He felt that the brain and Redeye were somehow monitoring him but swam on although the sun had risen and set several times. Eventually, he realised that he was approaching a large island and was confronted by massive cliffs, that soared up into the heavens, barring him from entry. Action had suffered many hours in the ocean and would not be defeated. He found the entrance to a small cove and waded into the small beach that it contained. He was amazed to find that there were small hairy creatures frolicking in the waters of the cove. One of them who seemed to be slightly larger than the others waved his elephantine trunk at him as a gesture of friendship. Action had decided that it was time for a more immediate response, and he would endeavour to climb the perpendicular cliffs that surrounded the island Luckily Action, was a superb athlete and had prodigious strength. He hurtled up the hitherto impassable barrier and cleared the final hurdle. Spread in front of him for mile after mile were fields of wildflowers that gave forth subtle perfumes of intense odours that satisfied the senses and left a permanent smile on the face."Lovely, isn't it?" the brain whispered in his ear.

"Yes, I can honestly say it's one of the most perfect areas that I have ever encountered, the only thing that ruined it was your spying activities," said Action.

"Yeah, sorry about that, but looking at the brighter side of things I am only looking after your best interests" smirked the brain.

"Do you realize just how much my prodigious swim and my mountaineering episode took, out of me.?"said Action.

Then gazing into the far distance, he picked out s vast lake that was fronted by a small hillock. A dense mist swirled over the lake which occasionally disappeared. The perfume of the tion's mind. Although he was gazing into the far distance he felt at wildflowers pervaded the whole area, leaving a soporific effect on Acpeace with the world. When he woke up, he realized that he had somehow lapsed into a catatonic trance. Yet even more bizarrely he had been out for the count for over a couple of hours. Then he shook his head and strode off in the direction of the distant lake. A voice in his ear admonished him that he was not going down the chosen path.

"Oh, it's not you again, I thought that I had shaken off the restricting shackles" complained Action.

"Well, it's certainly me again as you so tiresomely put. It and I am still looking after your best interests" confirmed the brain.

"Then you will have a long hike ahead of you, as I am heading for that distant lake. Action sensed that all, his movements were being monitored by another sauce, perhaps it was Redeye. He lengthened his stride and broke into a run. His stride altered yet again and he started to sprint.

"Why are we moving fast demanded a troubled voice?"

"Because the sooner we get there and carry out our investigation, the sooner we get back" replied Action.

"Ok, then we better get moving then" responded the brain.

"Well, for your personal edification, I have been hurtling along at vast speeds and have no intention of slowing down, I, therefore, find your comment of we better get moving most scurrilous" retorted Action.

Then Action lengthened his stride even further and began to fly in the direction of the distant lake... He was about halfway to his destination when an impenetrable fog descended on him cutting off all vision to the road ahead. He halted immediately and waited for the fog to clear.

"This is rather inconvenient don't blame you for stopping," said Redeye.

"I had this innate feeling that somehow you were stalking me" replied Action

"Yeah, you have always fascinated me with your constant dithering and changes of plan" continued Redeye.

"Well, you seem to be some kind of omnipotent creature with a vast understanding of the world around us. Perhaps, you can furnish me with information about our planet and our solar system?" Questioned Action.

"Delighted to do so" came the quick response.

"Legend has it that our planet is one of six planets. These planets have been named Earth, wind, fire water, iron, and Stone. Peculiarly enough all six planets have been gifted with vast quantities of all the six named ingredients. Why then have these planets been so named? The answer to that has been lost in the sands of time. Then your next question must be are there any other planets that are in other star systems? There again we have been advised that beyond our planets is only something that is known as the great darkness" replied Redeye.

"Then do you believe in all this nonsense and the great darkness?" demanded Action.

"Not in the slightest, it is all mumbo jumbo. I have immense powers and by concentrating can cause our planet to tilt. Therefore, I have negated the power of nature," said Redeye.

"Yes, I have to admit you seem to have obtained godlike powers," said Action.

"Then to allay, any suspicions you may have had of fraud I will demonstrate the power that I have garnered. For example, you are now sliding down a steep precipice, except you are not as I have just tilted the planet back to a stable position" said Redeye.

"That was absolutely amazing, I thought that I was just about to fall off the planet and the next instance the planet righted itself, although I still feel nauseous," said Action.

"That was an awful feeling that we encountered and thank God it's all over we never want to experience anything," said the brain.

"Just when I thought everything was getting better, you have popped up, yet again," said Action.

"If you wish I could dispose of this nuisance instantly," said Redeye.

"Actually, this nuisance as you so aptly describe him tends to keep me on my toes" replied Action.

"Then, if you don't require my assistance, I better attend to the many other many tasks that occupy me," said Redeye.

Then in the blink of an eye, he disappeared.

"Well, thank goodness that he has gone," said the brain.

"Let's face it, the major reason that you didn't like him was that he offered to exterminate you" replied Action.

Action discovered for the first time since he was de-jumbled that his thoughts were evolving loud and clear. Now for the first time, since he had been created, he had begun to feel something that was known as emotions. His investigation led him down the path of sadness and happiness. He didn't know how it happened, but suddenly his eyes filled with something known as tears. He felt incredibly unhappy as if his world had collapsed around him. Action now knew what the emotion of feeling sad and miserable was and felt extremely low.

He decided to try out the emotion of happiness, and almost immediately a feeling of contentment and joy seemed to enshroud him. This was bolstered by a wondrous calmness that informed him of the pure joy of life. Action now climbed to the top of the world and could do no wrong. He was totally entranced by the vision that spread before him of success and happiness. He then woke up from this reverie and smiled.

"Are you there brain? I am not sure what happened, but I seem to have been on a long journey between sadness and happiness. My emotions have been stretched to the limits and I am not sure whether to laugh or cry?" moaned Action.

"You have expressed my feelings exactly, although I listened in, I was totally confused by the outcome,"said the brain.

"Perhaps I can be of assistance?" chimed in a new voice.

"We're in the blue blazes did that voice come from. Questioned Action.

"Don't worry you can't see me, and you haven't gone blind. I am a volcano bubble left over from the last eruption,"said the voice.

"Well, that is an interesting concept, you are formed out of a volcanic explosion and are an invisible bubble"? questioned Action.

"Your summary is absolutely correct. However, added to this is my composition is that of the building blocks of life," said the voice.

"Well, we haven't been formally introduced but presumably you have a name? questioned Active.

"The only name I can think of with any relevance.is Bubbles" replied the voice.

"Ok then my invisible friend I shall call you Bubbles and will probably make you more visible," said Action.

The brain, which was infinitely more inquisitive than a brain should be, started to interrogate him.

"Do you really mean to tell me that this creature, whatever it was? Remained completely invisible to you" queried the brain.

"Astonishingly enough, that was perfectly true. He, she or whatever was invisible, her name was Bubble," said Action.

Oh, so she was feminine?" demanded the brain.

"With a name like Bubble, I most certainly would guess. so, and that would be my conjecture," said Action

The phantasma known as Bubble. seemed to have completely vanished, maybe she had been a figment of his imagination. He had no doubt that during the course of his long journey. he would encounter many more exotic and strange creatures

. Then, Action jumped high into the bright blue sky and pirouetted and screamed in delight, his reason being that he was free and able to do it. Then he sat down on a tree stump that had somehow magically appeared and pondered. He had realized that he was no longer in control of his own destiny. Whatever that meant?

His brain kept on persecuting him with asinine questions that were so numerous that he felt like punching himself on his head. However, he knew what the brain's response would be

"Why are you trying to hurt me, when, you will only injure yourself?"

Action decided that he would trek in the direction of the mighty volcano that lurked on the far horizon and was the birthplace of Bubbles. He had trekked quite a few miles when a huge chunk of carrion slammed into the path in front of him. Then the conveyor of this morbid cargo alighted in front of him. The creature was enormous and stank of putrefaction. Action was not in the habit of being bullied by s large overgrown vulture that stank of death. He picked up a large rock that lay in the path of the vulture and hurled it at the harbinger of death. He scored a direct hit on the Avion, which screeched in anger and flew off in the direction of the volcano. He then tramped onward to the volcano following the flight of the vulture. The temperature was now soaring and there was a constant bombardment of rocks from the angry mountain. The stink of hydrogen sulphide, an extremely poisonous gas, was unmistakable. As he neared the volcano there were numerous flights of the vulture type of bird hovering above him. However, having already put one of the carrion eaters to flight, he felt no fear of the foul birds.

The brain seemed to have departed for the moment, which he was quite glad. The volcano having been dormant for many years had decided to wake up. The complete mountain started to vibrate, and molten lava started pouring down the mountain in the direction of Action. He realized that he may have left it too late to avoid the disaster when he discovered that he was standing in the middle of a verdant meadow. Just how he had arrived there he hadn't an inkling.

"I was involved in my stalking act, and I realized that you had a real problem and were just about to be engulfed in the detritus of a volcano. So, I performed my godlike miracle and transported you here where you are out of harm's way" said Redeye.

Action stared incomprehensively at his saviour and wondered why.

The answer came back immediately from the thought of reading Redeye.

"Because I like you and you need me" was Redeye's response.

Action knew he had been deposited on a planet, where normal, laws often conflicted with what the planet's own rules and regulations. He realized that it may be necessary if he wished to survive to adjust to these strange new laws. Therefore, he surmised that Redeye could be also involved in his salvation. Perhaps there were many other strange creatures that he had yet to encounter.

Away from the blistering heat of the volcano and standing in the verdant meadows he felt completely relaxed. At the far end of the meadows, something bizarre seemed to be taking place. He could just make out what appeared to be a shimmering rainbow that flickered and disappeared before re-establishing itself in a blaze of colours. Action was striding quite fast towards the distant mirage as it began to register far more clearly. He could now make out that there were huge fountains that were obviously responsible for the rainbow conundrum. The fountains were enormous and were modelled on gigantic mythical animals, as he approached the fountains cautiously a bellow rang out.

"Don't be scared I am not going to hurt; you must be new around here"

Then to Action's utter astonishment, the smallest figure that he had ever seen appeared in front of him.

Because of the resonance of your powerful voice, I expected to meet up with a giant of a man," said Action.

"Well, I hope that you weren't too disappointed, by the way, my name is large"

"Yeah, what's in a name any way you can't judge a book by its cover" Action replied.

"Very amusing, although I am not certain why?" replied Large.

"Never mind, I am sure that you will discover the answer in a couple of hundred years" quipped Action.

"That is a very unfair comment I will be dead and buried by then" retorted Large.

"Well, you are meeting up with some extremely strange and bizarre characters. This fellow with a foghorn voice is a typical example of an individual with an enormous complex. He endeavours to hide his diminutive stature by calling himself Large" Said. the brain

"Oh, I wondered when you would appear again no doubt you have been sniffing around spying on all and sundry" replied Action.

"Now that you mentioned it, I have seen you hobnobbing with that rather large gentleman with the Redeye," said the brain.

"This is a prime example of your exceedingly furtive behaviour. You really are turning into a sneaking individual" retorted Action.

"You certainly have been a medalling individual with no sympathy for others and I take grave exception to, your asinine comments if I so wished to do so I could blast you out of existence" boomed out Redeye.

"However, you won't do that because Action is your pet project and if you do blast me out of existence, he goes as well" smirked the brain.

"Yeah, but I do have another option of corrective surgery I may be able to remove a parasite such as you without damaging the host," said Redeye.

"That would be far too risky, one slip of the surgical blade and your project is doomed" replied the brain.

"Hold on a minute, don't I have any say in the matter" interjected Action.

"No, you have no say whatsoever in the matter as you are the route of the problem," said Redeye.

"I have a solution to this problem, why don't we toss a coin? Then if the coin comes up heads, I will take the surgery. if not, I will wait and see what happens to me," said Action.

"Well, I have to say you are a very brave thingy and I have the utmost respect for your courage," said Redeye

The coin was then tossed up in the air and landed face down.so there was no need for surgery.

Action surmised that he was bored, he wasn't quite certain what the term meant but he associated it with doing nothing. He felt that indolence was not for him, and he ought to express himself as a vibrant being. He took up double marathon running, which he found quite rewarding but still completed the course ahead of his competitors by a couple of hours. What could he do to allay his boredom? His next venture was balloon racing which jerked him high into the atmosphere and hurtled him at a terrifying speed at vast mountains. Amazingly he encountered Bubble who was intent on rushing through the sky as if he hadn't a care in the world. But at least through his extremely dangerous and hazardous sports, he was no longer bored. Peculiarly enough he hadn't had any encounters with either the brain or Redeye.

However, Action's luck didn't last forever

"Well, I thought that I had better check you out and see how you are?" rang out the booming voice of Redeye.

"Thank you very much for your enquiry but I am feeling quite chipper, although I have been doing rather a lot of exercise" replied Action.

"I know you have I have been watching you" replied Redeye.

"So, at last, you have caught up with your pet project,"said the smarmy voice of the brain.

There was a large flash, and the voice of the brain was no more.

"What have you done have you destroyed the brain?" questioned Action.

"Certainly nothing as diabolical as that. All that I did was transport him to an echo chamber. We all know how he loves the sound of his own voice, he will be very happy there," said Redeye.

"Well, at least you got rid of him I was getting very fed up with him droning on about me being your pet project. I suppose that there is no truth in his statement."Queried Action.

"In my pet projects?" replied None whatsoever I am a god why would I indulge in such petty trivialities," said Redye.

Out in the distant realms of the universe, a trillion light years from anywhere. There existed an omnipotent god with amazing powers that harboured the power of creation. However, at an early stage of his creations, he listened to wise advice from Action and the brain. We wish them every success and a long and fruitful existence.

ORIGINAL WORLDS BOOK TWO

SLUGGISH BEHAVIOUR

Where was he, he didn't actually know. His vision seemed to be impaired by strange wavy tendrils that were constantly bidding him adieu, He dragged himself along and felt very sluggish, which was peculiar because that was what he was a slug. However, having been born on the planet Zog, he was no ordinary slug and was over two hundred feet long and weighed in at a spectacular ten tons, His habitat was a swamp that housed some savage creatures within it. There were certain areas in the swamp that he stayed well clear of, mostly the salty areas, and still had no inkling why he did so. Then an important recollection hunted him down. He remembered a gigantic explosion that dismembered the planet that he was created on. Then being. hurled far out into space, after that his mind went blank and his memory was zero. Something that was large and green scuttled across the path in front of him. He carried on his mission regardless of all interruptions that nature through in his way. What was his mission? He hadn't a clue, but it was obviously very important. A massive. black splodge smashed into the ground in front of him and Slug, that was what he had decided to call himself, as he was a slug. He knew instantly the name of the creature that had landed on the path in front of him it was a Tree Toad., they were also known sometimes as suicide toads. The reason for this was that they climbed into the highest branches of the trees and waited for their prey to arrive and smashed down on it. Unfortunately, quite often they missed their proposed victims entirely and committed harikari., hence the name of suicide toads The situation became even weirder when it was revealed that they didn't regard their proposed victims as sustenance as they never intended to eat them.

However, Slug was completely disinterested in the eating habits of Tree Toads. and carried on with his journey, Slug also knew that he would possibly encounter far more dangerous creatures than death-seeking Tree Toads. Slug rounded the next bend in the path and almost barged into the creature in front of him. She was beautiful and had transfixed him with wonderful plumage. The problem was that Slug. couldn't identify what type of avian she was except that she was drop, dead gorgeous

Then a voice seemed to arrive out of the ether.

"Well, this. is an unexpected surprise, you are huge and. very black. What kind of species are you?" demanded the avian.

"I am a slug and am trying to find my way through life," said Slug.

"Then as introductions seem to be in order, I am called Paradise," said the avian and fluttered her feathers in an alluring way.

"Yeah, you really are a fascinating and beautiful creature, and I would be delighted if our paths headed in the same direction" replied Slug.

"Flattery and good manners are essential in travel today and obviously you have mastered both. However, as you have not been gifted with the power of flight I will fly on ahead and warn you of any dangers that you may encounter," said Paradise

Then having been notified about his early warning system Slug continued his arduous and tortuous journey to wherever he was going. Flying above him and constantly notifying him of any danger that may be ahead was his constant companion Paradise.

She then swooped down on the path and landed in front of him, forcing him to stop.

"There is a huge nasty nasty-looking monster in front of you, my advice is to approach it with caution" advised Paradise.

Having digested this advice, Slug slowed down and in doing so encountered a violent bend in the path which caused him to halt immediately and there blocking his path was one of the most grotesque creatures that he had ever encountered. It was covered with scales of a yellowish hue and stank of putrification and vomit.

"Well, look what's just arrived on the scene and just in time for my lunch, but having said that it is far too large and is probably indigestible" moaned the monster.

"Yeah, you would certainly have had a problem trying to eat me I am at least four times larger than you, and if you didn't smell so offensive I would take great delight in covering and squashing you," said Slug.

In the meantime, Paradise had come to inspect the monster. However, she had taken off again almost immediately, saying she couldn't stand the smell.

Slug had had enough of the stinking, monster that had invaded his world and without hesitation, he was on his way.. `

However, his constant companion Paradise, still hovered above his head. Eventually, Slug decided that he would halt his journey for a few moments and slithered on top of a tree trunk that was sprawled across his route and blocking his way. Paradise then swooped down and joined him. Then, a beautiful yellow butterfly hovered above the tree trunk and then descended. Paradise moved like lightning and gulped down the butterfly in one swift movement.

"What possessed you to destroy a beautiful creature?" Slug demanded

"Delicious" was Paradise's only response.

Slug realized that he and Paradise had formed a symbiotic relationship, and he didn't want to jeopardize this by taking the matter further. They continued their journey with Paradise still acting as the spy in the sky. However, their progress became far more arduous as they continued through the swampland. Their greatest problem by far was the massive trees that had become uprooted, because of the swampy conditions and slowed down all progress. Slug was becoming very disillusioned, because of the slow progress, when Paradise swooped down on the path in front of him. causing him to stop immediately.

"I have encountered a huge problem ahead of us, the path is now entirely. blocked by huge misshapen creatures," said Paradise.

"Then, what exactly do these creatures look like?" Demanded Slug.

"Well, I can give a rough description which will, be terribly precise" replied Paradise

"OK carry on a rough description will certainly suffice,"said Slug.

"Both of them have a single horn in front of them, which must be at least twenty meters long. Their tails like most of their body are scaled and have a huge spike on their tails."Said Paradise.

"You can stop there. I know exactly what they are, you have no need to continue,"said Slug.

"Then enlighten me what are they? questioned Paradise"

"They may look quite ferocious but are actually quite harmless and in fact are beasts of burden" replied Slug.

"What is a beast of burden?" inquired Paradise.

Put very simply, it is a creature that carries something on behalf of others. Now tell me where there. other creatures involved?"Asked Slug.

"Yeah, there were four others that controlled these beasts of burden, and they were humanoids. However, we won't have any problems with them as I will use my mind-bending powers to control the humanoids,"said Paradise.

"Then please tell me what are mind-bending powers and how do they function?"Asked a bemused Slug

"To borrow your. phrase. Put very simply I am utilizing the power of my mind to bend those humanoids to obey my every command," said Paradise,

"Well, that must be quite something I can't wait to witness your performance," said Slug.

Just a couple of hours later Slug's wish materialized. Paradice had stationed herself on a lofty branch overlooking the area where the beasts of burden functioned, in the meantime, Paradice had found out what the beasts were actually called. Because of their appearance, they were called Single hornbills. However, she did feel that although they may have had a peaceful demeanour, they did have a ferocious appearance. She concentrated on the four humanoids that had appeared alongside the beasts. Her desire was to clear the blockage that was impeding their journey. Therefore, into the minds of the humanoids she sent an urgent command to drive the Single hornbills forward and release the blockage. Paradice's efforts paid dividends as the beasts were prodded and hit and forced to move forward. Then, eventually, the slow progress before turned itself into a stampede that crushed one of the humanoids and died on the spot. However, their passage forward was no longer blocked.

"Yeah, there is no doubt about it, your mind-controlling effort worked an absolute treat," said Slug.

"Yes, I suppose that congratulations are in order, and we will be now able to move on to wherever we are going" replied Paradice.

"Do you know something I am becoming quite enamoured with you. Yet I know that it is an impossibility with you as I am a massive Slug, and you are a beautiful avian" said Slug.

"This might not be a problem as I am able to use my mind to transport you to any venue that may desire," said Paradise.

"That sounds wonderful. However, we have a long journey to complete wherever we are going. So, I better not make an immediate decision," said Slug.

Then having clarified his position both of them set off to their unknown destination and as usual Paradise was scanning the sky ahead of them searching for any impending danger. Slug was becoming very frustrated by the terrible terrain that he had to keep pulling his massive body through. Then there was a terrific thud as his lady lone crash-landed on the path in front of him.

"What in the blue blazes is happening? demanded Slug.

"Well, I was flying quite high g in the sky when this enormous black bird attacked me,"said Paradice.

"I most certainly did not attack you I was endeavouring to converse with you when you panicked and fled,"said a voice from a tree above them. By the way, my name is Jacob,"said the voice

Slug looked up and spotted a massive black bird in the tree above him.

"Okay, I may have been a trite hasty, but I was sure that you were, about to attack me" apologized Paradise

"No problem, I know that I appear rather large and scary, but I assure you that I am a gentle and cool avian," said Jacob.

"Then what kind of avian are you?" inquired Slug.

"I am a supercharged vulture, but you call me Jacob."

He then continued"I am not certain in which direction you are traveling but you are very much down there and we including your lady are up here. If I can assist you in any way with your travels as I am large and scary, I am your man," said Jacob.

"Well, as far as I am concerned the more the merrier,"said Paradice.

"Then we are agreed and there is no need to sign on the dotted line. So, the journey begins" said Slug.

Then, as they set off on their travels they became totally confused, whereas previously there had been only two of them, now there were three. Slug continued on with his nightmare journey smashing his way through dense forest and saturated swamp, whilst flying above him. Using the freedom of the air, were his two companions. However, as there was no day or night on planet Zog, only perpetual day, very often the two avians flew down to keep him company after his tedious journey through the swamp. The trio faced their first serious encounter and flew down in order to recount their experience.

"Neither Jacob nor I were entirely sure about the breed of bird that we encountered, what we did find out was that they were ferocious and attacked us without any provocation. The bad news is that there were hundreds of them, the good news is that they were minute. Jacob succeeded. in knocking hundreds out of the sky"'s aid Paradice.

"Well done Jacob"was Slug's only comment.

"We have a nasty feeling, that they may have tried to follow us back," said Paradice.

"Good, I will be waiting for them and give them a huge hiding,"said Slug.

Just then a noisy squawking squad of miniature birds, known as Pirate birds, descended through the trees and instantly attacked their cowering prey. This was a very bad mistake for the Pirate birds as a huge two-hundred-foot monster launched himself at them and annihilated hundreds of them in one fell swoop.

"That was incredible, you smote those hounds of hell, with the fist of justice," said Paradice.

"Yeah, regarding your comment it was very poetic although am not too certain what it means?" replied Slug.

"You are my eternal hero and can do no wrong and I want to combine with you and have your babies,"said Paradice.

"Then, I will give you the same reply that I gave you as last time I would like to think about it" replied Slug

"Then don't think about it forever, as actions speak louder than words," said Jacob.

"I will bear that in mind, the next time that I thump you" replied a caustic Slug.

Just a few hours later, they were still discussing their victory over the Pirate birds. However, Slug was. becoming extremely bored by the repetition that kept on occurring in the conversation. In his boredom, he lashed out at the massive pile of logs that were sprawled across the path in all directions. When a massive two-hundred-foot monster kicks a pile of logs it spears them across vast tracks of land. However, as if by magic a large brown sack appeared Paradice swept into the air and hovered above the sack before descending. She then opened the sack and let out a wild whoop of delight.

"This is absolutely incredible the sack is stuffed full of gold coins. The majority of which seem to be King Ghophis the second. coinage. We are rich beyond our wildest dreams" said Paradice.

"My dreams are far richer than bags of gold coins" mumbled Slug.

"Then, what are we going to do with this vast wealth that we have so miraculously acquired?" said Jacob.

"Do you know, I am beginning to think that this latest episode is my fault entirely if I hadn't kicked that pile of logs in a fit of pique, we wouldn't have discovered all that gold. Therefore, my suggestion must be. that we bury the gold and leave it for the less fortunate to find," said Slug.

"That is very commendable. and I totally concur," said Jacob.

"Then, I suppose that I must agree also, although I do think that the gold may be very useful at a later date," said Paradice.

"Well, then I suggest that we should carry on with our great adventure of exploration and discovery," said Slug.

Then having carefully reburied the sack of gold they continued their journey of exploration. Just as before the avians acted as Slug's early warning system should there be any approaching danger. Paradice was far more the frequent visitor as she still, felt a great yearning for Slug. However, Jacob loved the freedom of the sky and enjoyed the company of his pretty avian companion Paradice. Everything seemed to be behaving well until an ominous black cloud appeared in the distance and seemed to be heading directly for the two avians. They stopped in mid-flight to discuss the approaching enigma.

"This cloud seems to have a sinister aspect about it. It is moving at a tremendous speed toward us, yet it doesn't seem to have any exterior means of propulsion?" said Jacob.

"What shall we do then, wait here and wait for it to devour us or like hell and try to get away from it?" said Paradice.

However, the choice was entirely removed from their hands when the black cloud ran them over.

A disembodied voice from nowhere immediately apologized.

"Sorry about that, I was going too fast and entirely misjudged the distance and ran you over. I have turned into a bit of a cloud hog," said the voice.

Both Paradice and Jacob were aware at the same time that they were being addressed by an impossibly tall individual. who was hopping from foot to foot in nervous trepidation.

"Then who are you? I must admit that I have never been run over by a cloud hog before," said Jacob.

"Then, my sincere apologies yet again, and for your further edification I am Professor Knowitall" replied the impossibly tall man.

Then the professor began to boast about the superiority of his race and the massive strides that they had made in inventing amazing inventions, his race was called. The Strident as they intended to reign supreme among the many Galaxies. Paradice had taken an instant dislike to the professor who was incredibly proud of his race's extraordinary invention achievements. They had even invented time travel, which turned out to be a complete disaster as they succeeded in losing a couple of their race both in the past and in the future. There had been no recovery process formulated and they were forced to abandon them there. He then demonstrated the horrendous weapons of the future with which they. would pulverize worlds if they didn't submit to The Strident's aggression. Both Pradice and Jacob were very dismayed by the boastful and aggressive behaviour that seemed to be permanently on his agenda.

"Well, professor I take grave exception. to your race's domineering behaviour," said Paradise.

"Oh yeah, and what are you intending to do about it?" sneered the professor.

"As you have asked, I will demonstrate exactly what I intend to do about it?" replied Paradice.

She then concentrated all her efforts on bending the professor's mind to obey her commands, as he was a humanoid she knew that he would not be able to resist her commands. She ordered him to face her and clasp his hands as if in prayer.

"You are completely under my control and will obey all my commands. Now bend forward clasp your ankles and stand on one leg.

This was of course an impossible command and he fell over with a mighty crash and lay on the floor groaning with pain. Because of the fall, the professor was Jared back into instant consciousness

"What happened, where have I been?" was the professor's only comment

"You have been on a journey of rehabilitation and will attempt to. negate. the power of. the horrific. Weaponry of Strident. Now repeat what I have just said word perfect" said Paradice.

"I have been on a journey of rehabilitation and will attempt to negate the power of the horrific weaponry of Strident," said the professor.

"Well done professor, that was a perfect recapitulation of everything that I said" replied a smiling Paradice.

"Do you surmise, that there is any chance of success, in your brainwashing ability??" questioned Jacob.

"To be quite honest, I haven't a clue, but it was certainly worth trying," said Paradice.

Just then the professor made a grunting noise and seemed to be emerging from his trance.

"Well, that was thoroughly invigorating, and I feel totally refreshed and I feel that a great weight has been lifted off my mind,"said the professor.

"Then presumably it has changed the ideology that guides you?" queried Jacob.

"Exactly, have you been reading my mind? asked the professor.

Jacob just grinned at him and didn't reply.

You see I have changed all my ideas of dominating other civilizations and feel that we must adapt to each other's needs and live in peace and tranquility," said the professor

"Then how do you intend to dismantle the weaponry?" inquired Jacob.

"There will not be the slightest problem with that, as I invented most of the weapons in the first place following the invitation of the generals at Strident. However, early on in my career, I was a pacifist and was highly suspicious of the approach made to me to construct the ultimate weapon. So, although I provided the ultimate weapon. I also installed a fail-safe device within it. Therefore, at the press of a button within this ship, I can disable the complete arsenal of Strident,"said the professor.

"Do you know Professor, not only did I not trust you, but I also didn't like you. However, it now appears that I have misjudged you, and from now I shall have the greatest respect and admiration for you" said Paradice

"Yeah, I think that I better descend and inform my love partner of the latest happenings said Paradice.

Then having swooped down and informed Slug of all the recent events, he was completely astounded. Then, to add to his amazement he found that his massive two-hundred-foot body was rising from the forest floor until he was hovering just outside the professor's spaceship.

"What in the blue blazes is happening I seem to be levitating," said a distraught Slug.

Then the professor appeared hovering alongside Slug.

"I am dreadfully keen for snatching you away from whatever you were doing but I have heard so much about you that I thought that I better make your acquaintance," said the professor.

"Well ditto, I have heard an amazing amount about you, and especially how you changed direction from being one of the bad guys to being a superhero," said Slug.

"I am not sure about the sobriquet of the superhero, just I knew that I made the correct choice between war and peace" replied the professor.

A billion light years from a planet known as Earth on a planet called Zog. There existed two creatures, a Slug, and an Avian. Then because of the extreme dangers that they both encountered both fell in love with each other. However, there was a major problem facing them should they ever want children. Slug was over two hundred feet in length whereas his pretty Avian love was a mere five feet tall. The height difference was obviously a serious difficulty. Then, they had an encounter with a professor who entirely changed their lives. Therefore, if your faster-than-light ship is in the vicinity of planet Zog pop in and see them as I am sure that they would make you most welcome. ad infinitum.

DRAGON FIRE

Well, he was somewhat confused and didn't even know his gender although he felt like he was a male. He was not even certain How he had been created or what the term created signified. Another strange thing seemed to be happening to him, he seemed to be flying, yet there again he wasn't certain if he was using the correct terminology. He flapped his massive wings and realized that he must be flying. Everything seemed to be flashing into the brain in rapid succession. and analysed the meaning of his existence. He seemed to be able to control his flight path. and headed towards a planet that loomed up in front of him. He glided. down to the planet but misjudged his descent and crashed into a large boulder that impeded any further progress. The light that was shining from the boulder was unremitting in its intensity and furnished him with a mirror image of himself. He stared at his reflection both in wonder and awe. He was absolutely gigantic and shiny scales encompassed the complete stretch of his body. This creature that dominated his reflection what was it and what was its function? He flapped his enormous wings and soared up into the burning air of the planet, he flapped them again to cool himself off. He then decided to try something completely different. The reason is that inside himself was a Firey something that wanted to escape. He therefore held his breath and concentrated on what seemed to be an eternity then came welling up inside until it exploded. With a great spurt of fire. The incandescent flame sliced into the mirror image on the boulder and reduced it to a dried-up heap of rubble.

`Then a voice thundered down from the heavens.

"Success complete success, I have created my own Dragon, and I shall call it, George," said the voice

"Excuse me but don't I have any say in the matter," said the newly named George

"No, you most certainly do not. I have spent several lifetimes searching for. old Dragon eggs to fabricate my pet little monster," said the voice.

"Well, that is interesting, that means that there are others of my kind and yes you can call me George"

There was an ominous silence, whilst the voice considered his options.

"I must apologize for my previous comment. I gave the impression that I would be rearing my own pet little monster. However, having now viewed your gargantuan size I now realize that my idea small pet is totally absurd," said the voice.

"Yeah, at least it now seems that I may have relatives, and just for the record what is your name?" queried George

"Well, I am known by many different names. However, I will give you a point in the right direction. I am named after a four-legged friend but spelled backward," said the voice

"Then, I comprehend your problem in its entirety. There are a multitude of false gods stretching far back into antiquity. You, however, have a great deal of charisma surrounding you that is enhanced by having an exceedingly loud voice," said George.

"OK, then how would you like me to call you?" said George.

"To be totally honest I would prefer if you called me by my proper name" the voice responded.

"Your wish is my command, but what exactly do your powers consist of?" questioned George

"I am completely omnipotent and all-powerful. Can either destroy worlds or make them prosper, very often it's the choice of the inhabitants of these planets whether they wish to survive or not," said God.

"Still more intriguing must be the search for my relatives, is it possible that there are still surviving Dragons" questioned George

"I can honestly promise you that there are no more Dragons. The reason is that a couple of thousand years ago, Dragons were very numerous but sought grandeur above their station. Enormous armies of Dragons fought each other, and vast tracks of land were scorched into oblivion. They didn't realize that I even existed Eventually I became frustrated and decided to put an end to all the barbarity and bullying that for the most part had been endured by the humanoids seemed to me that the only answer must be to destroy the whole of the dragon race which I duly did wiping them off the face of the planet" said God.

"Believe it or not, I fully understand your reason for erasing the Dragons from the face of the planet," said George

"Then you have obtained wisdom far beyond your tender years" replied God.

Just a few hours later George was celebrating the joy and freedom of life by performing intricate movements in the burning heavens above the planet. He was also scanning the planet for any sign of life but apart from the occasional humanoid, there was a scarcity of living entities. However, he had just made a sweep over a rocky cliff face when he received a signal that there was another Dragon in close proximity to him. George landed a short distance from where he had picked up the signal. He then strode to a cavern entrance where the signal was emanating from. He then entered the cavern which was vast and seemed to carry on forever. There was then a flash and a small perfectly formed Dragon made her appearance, a voice then entered George's head

"You have come at last, and I have been waiting for you for centuries. I am called Twinkle" she said

She then went on to explain her birth and heritage.

"Thousands of years ago, we endured internecine conflict in something that became known as the Dragon Wars.

Both my mother and father remained neutral during these terrible times and wished that peace and prosperity would return across all Dragon nations. This unfortunately never happened and so my parents planned to place me in a secure and safe place, and this cavern is where you found me, my parents are dead and long gone, and yet somehow, I knew that somebody would free me from eternal loneliness," said Twinkle.

"Yeah, what a history of trial and tribulation you have endured but the good news is that I am here to rescue you from eternal loneliness," said a smiling George.

"By the way, I forgot to ask but can you fly?" said George.

Twinkle responded instantly by shooting up and down the cavern at prodigious speed and then replied.

"Yes, I can fly".

George then jetted up into the sky, closely followed by his Dragon Lady. As she had been enclosed in the cavern for an incredibly long time, he thought that it would be only fair, if he took her on a sightseeing tour of the planet. They hurtled into the blazing sky which was dominated by an enormous solar object called Sol. Unlike other planets in other solar systems, there was perpetual daylight in perpetuity. They flew over raging torrents of water that cascaded down the mountainside to crash into a large lake that acted as a receptacle for the torrential water. They passed over jagged peaks that seemed to be insistent in piercing the billowing rain clouds that threatened the constantly swamped terrain.

George decided that having shown Twinkle the marvels of the planet, he would descend and converse with her., Twinkle had the same idea and perched herself on the same ridge beside him.

"Well, you certainly showed me a fantastic glimpse of the wonders of this planet, and we had a whirlwind tour. So, thank you," said Twinkle.

The next moment there was a boom of thunder and a flash of lightning

"Greetings, and congratulations on surviving the war I am sorry about your parents," said a booming voice.

"Who is this and why is he sorry about my parents?" questioned Twinkle.

"Well, extraordinary enough he is God, and because of the Dragon wars he found it necessary to exterminate your parents, but don't feel too bad about it as he has already apologized about it and he cares about everyone," said George.

"That is absolute rubbish. if he cared for everyone did, he exterminate my parents?" demanded Twinkle

The booming voice came again from the sky

"You have every reason to vilify me, and I can only apologize yet again if you had witnessed the callous way in which the Dragons slaughtered all opposition on both sides of the conflict you would realize the difficult decision that I had to make," said God

Then, having witnessed God's departure. Both flew off in continuance of their exploration of the planet. Unfortunately. Because of the high winds raging against them. they had to descend to a lower level to seek sanctuary. They found themselves in a deep valley that was protected on all sides

"What are your aims in life?" Twinkle asked.

"I am not too certain as I have only just been created" replied George

"Well, I know exactly how my life will be planned I want to have hundreds of babies," said Twinkle.

"Then who do you intend to have all those babies with as there doesn't seem to be many male Dragons around"? asked George.

"Think of yourself as being incredibly lucky I have selected you as the Dragon of my dreams" replied Twinkle

George decided to succumb to his preordained fate, besides which he found her incredibly attractive.

The one thing that kept George's concentration at a high level was when he decided to create First of all he would take a huge breath whilst breathing in, this had the effect of allowing him to kindle the huge fire that burned within his massive chest. Then by expelling fire from his throat, he was able to cause a massive conflagration. However, George had no intention of using his fire-breathing exploits for any clandestine exploits.

Twinkle kept popping in and using any excuse to see him

"Don't you. Think that it is about time we should have our babies?" She said on one occasion but all he replied was

"Life must go on"

"Why are you spending all your time annihilating a non-existent foe? Twinkle asked him.

"I have to be prepared for all eventualities"was George's instant response

"Then, possibly you have lost you have lost your sex drive?" said Twinkle

"That is a distinct possibility if I knew what a sex drive was?" replied George

Twinkle stormed out in a rage and then kept thinking that there may be another Dragon somewhere. That may understand her better.

Then peculiarly enough God decided to play his hand.

"Twinkle as is my prerogative; I have been monitoring your predicament. As I understand it your problem is that you want to have lots of babies. But unfortunately, lover, boy George, doesn't give you the time of day" concluded God

"Listen as far as I am concerned it is a matter that concerns the two of us and I would prefer it you didn't meddle in matters that don't concern you" chided Twinkle.

" You do realize that I am a God, and I could force George to give you babies if you so wished it"replied God.

"Do you know something that is far more important than you could offer me that is free will and I can't take that away from George" explained Twinkle

"You have explained your reasons clearly and succinctly and with that in mind I will abide by your decision," said God,

Twinkle didn't bother to tell George about her brief encounter with God and carried on with her normal chores. Until one day something unexpected happened, a huge creature appeared on the horizon and headed in her direction. She was so alarmed by the size of the creature that she sent an urgent message to George. Amazingly enough, both he and God arrived at the same time

It's a Blatherspot roared out God, they are nasty spikey creatures who have only one objective to stab you to death.

"Then how do we defeat this evil beast?" demanded George.

"You possess the one thing that they detest, the gift of fire," said God.

"I know that you have been practicing for ages and now you have the chance to prove that you are a hero," said God.

As soon as he heard God's proclamation, George hurtled into the sky above the planet toward the Blatherspot. He circled in the sky above the creature, obviously planning his attack. Then at high speed, he swooped down on his target. George opened his jaws and a vast cloud of fire jetted toward the Blatherspot encased in an incandescent embrace the vast creature started to shudder as if it was being afflicted by some terrible disease it began to inflate at an enormous size and still continued to expand. Then it stopped expanding. and although it was a prodigious size it commenced to shudder much more violently than the previous time. Then it halted all motion and time stood still. Then a vast explosion tore through the planet's atmosphere and blackened the sky.

The immediate effect of the explosion was huge chunks of stinking black matter were hurled into the air and then rained down on the planet.

George's only comment was

"Good riddance"

Sparkle endorsed this remark with

"You were quite correct in your comment that you have to be prepared for all eventualities," said Sparkle

"I think that I must thank you, God, for your information on how we could destroy the monster. How did you know that fire was its weak point?" inquired George

"I didn't know it was a complete guess, but at least it gave you the confidence to fight the beast" replied God.

"Yeah, it certainly gave me the confidence I will give you that, but I suppose it could have easily gone the other way," said George.

"No, that would. not have been a happy ending," said Twinkle.

After George's tryst with the Blatherspot and having recovered from his near-death experience decided to take an easier approach to life. Twinkle was still infatuated with the huge dragon and used any excuse to make an impromptu visit to see him. However, her real reason for constant visits was her yearning to give birth to a baby dragon

George on the other hand was quite content to meander onwards to his unknown destination. Then a crisis arose from a totally different direction. George had just finished a random target practice by shooting streams of fire at a rock face when the booming voice of God entered his mind

"I came as soon as I found out the decision they made," said God.

"What in tarnation are you talking about?" questioned George

"Well, I haven't been totally honest with you," said God.

"So, ok, what have you been misleading me about? I am sure it is not the first time," said George

"The problem is that I am not the only God that rules this planet. There are three gods and we have always been fair in our dealings with each other. However, because of recent actions by a certain large dragon known as George. You have loomed large and clear in the eyes of the other two gods," said God

"Well, this really a set of extraordinary circumstances. What do you suggest that I should do and what are the other gods' intentions?" asked George

I really believe that this problem has arisen out of jealousy," said God.

"Then, I wouldn't believe that this would be at all believable, you are telling me that gods have feelings," said George

"Oh, that is a common misconception, of course, gods have feelings" replied God

"Tell me more" urged George

"Very well, I have always been on the same planet, pardon the pun, as Nik the other god. However, Jaz the other god is a twisted glory-seeking nobody" snarled God

"You don't like him do you" smirked George

"No, I wouldn't give him a brass farthing, whatever that may be," shouted God

"Do you know, you haven't told me what this Jaz fellow wants?"Said George

"Your right I didn't did I? he wants you" shouted God.

"What do you, mean he wants me" shouted George

"Don't worry he can't have you reared from an egg,"said God

"You still haven't told me, what he wants me for?" questioned George

"No, I haven't have I. He wants to put you on display

"What do you mean by that comment?" demanded George

"Well. Jaz has grand ideas far above his station he has dreams of being a promoter and you will function as the main figure in his display as a real live fire-breathing dragon. His grand idea is to build an arena, which will be easy enough for him he will just imagine it and it will exist," said God.

"How does he construct something from thin air? That is impossible?" queried George

"No, it is not impossible for him, Jaz is a god just like me and everything is possible,"said God

"Well, I must admit, that I wouldn't like to be at the centre of Jaz's freak show."You obviously detest him, and no doubt have formulated a plan to frustrate him?" said d George

"Yeah, how right you are Jaz thinks that I will hand over the dragon egg that I have loved and nurtured, that is you, George, he will have another agender when I finish with him,"said God.

It became completely obvious over the next few days, that Jaz's one desire was to become a master impresario. He even approached George, who would be the star of his show, with the offer of providing him with great riches. At the instigation of God, George said that he would give it serious consideration.

The arena was as massive as Jaz's ego and would seat at least twenty thousand. The majority of the occupants would be humanoid. Jez then became involved in the creation of mythical beasts, many of which were ferocious-looking but lacked charisma. Jaz's attempts at creating weird and wonderful beasts had turned out to be a series of dismal flops..

George was half expecting a visit from a gloating God and as always, his expectations turned into reality.

"Well, I had a sneaking suspicion that this excuse for a God would fall flat on his face how right I was. However, just to make sure I have put the second part of my plan into action" smirked God.

"Ok, I hear you loud and clear, and what exactly does the second part of your plan entail"demanded George

"Well, tomorrow I am attending a dinner to celebrate the success of Jaz's enormous project, and needless to say there will only be the three of us there. My idea will be that will poison him. black venom," said God.

"Isn't that a bit extreme? will it kill him?" asked a perturbed George

" There is absolutely no chance that Gods are immortal and can't die, although he may feel pretty lousy for a couple of days" replied God

"Then, won't either of your God buddies be a tad suspicious?" asked George.

"Yes, I should think that Jaz will be highly suspicious, but Nick will be highly supportive," said God

Then, as usual, God performed one of his vanishing acts, and George and Twinkle didn't hear from him for a couple of days. Then, when he finally made contact. Again, heralded by the sound of his penetrative voice, it was only then that George realized something that he had never seen God in the flesh. Although weirdly enough he thought that he knew him quite well. Therefore, he thought that he would bring up the subject to God.

"Well, I have left you both alone for a couple of days to give you both time to gather your thoughts, but before I start would you like to question me on any subject?" said God.

"Yeah, I most certainly would. It occurred to me that you have been represented to us as a disembodied loud voice. What exactly is your physical appearance What do you look, like?"Demanded George.

"OK, don't be worried about my physical appearance, remember I am a God, so it is hardly the norm,"said God.

In the next instant, a huge blue figure appeared before them and indulged itself in a courteous wave

Is that really you?"Asked George.

"Yeah, it is certainly me"the blue figure responded.

"Then I am most impressed by your massive biceps"retorted George

"Thank you for the compliment. I work out a fair amount and bench press two huge mountains,"said God.

"That sounds totally too strenuous for me. I will give that type of workout a miss," said George

"Then perhaps you can tell me what happened at the feast of the Gods?"Queried George.

"Well, to be honest, Jez was so embarrassed with his foolish attempt to become an impresario that I felt quite sorry for him," said God.

"Does that mean that you felt so sorry for him that you no longer had any intention of poisoning him?"Questioned George

"No, it didn't put me off at all I still poisoned him. I might have felt sorry for him but I didn't like him, so I poisoned him."Said God

"What effect did it have on him?" asked George

Yeah, it was actually far more than I expected. He stood up and then rolled on the ground clutching himself as if he was experiencing extreme agony," said God.

"Then what happened"demanded George

"He stood up laughing and said that he knew that I had tried to poison him?"

"That had the instant effect of me hating him even more,"said God.

"Nick then intervened on my behalf and asked him what proof of the poisoning. However, I knew that wouldn't be a problem as black venom is completely untraceable. Then Nick became furious with Jaz and accused him of making ridiculous accusations against me without any foundation. He then launched into a diatribe against Jaz accusing him of trying to take the limelight off himself because of his failed arena project. They both ended up shouting at each other and Jaz stormed out," said God.

"Then, where exactly does that leave us?" asked George.

"Well, put it like this, Jaz appears to have alienated two Gods who have the power to halt any major schemes that he might have wished to bring to fruition,"said God.

"Then. you seem to have smashed the idea of me being the major player in the arena but thank you as I don't think that it was right for me," said George.

Twinkle, who had been listening to, the conversation breathed a sigh of relief, as she didn't want the love of her life embroiled in any spurious contest that was of no consequence.

Then the love of her life turned his gaze onto her, and she felt a tremor of desire invade her whole being.

"Well, I suppose that you have been very patient and waited a long time to cuddle a dragon egg and I think that this should be the moment when we make mad passionate love

Twinkle gazed at her own armoured coated dragon whose scales shimmered in the half-light. He advanced toward her and wrapped his huge, scaled body round her, and entwined himself with her. There was no music, but they made their own music that conveyed them both into fantasy land. Faster and faster. with little chance of the pace ever abating. Fire flickered across their scaled bodies as the gyrations increased so did their lovemaking. The excitement for both was frantic and amazing. Then the music in their blended minds slowed to an intimate bonding between both of them. This was a blazing inferno of Dragon love and a journey between the stars. Where was this music of their minds coming from? They didn't know and didn't care as long as it still carried on.

Then at last exhausted and sated from their. Frantic endeavours they collapsed on the ground in a heap of sexual enjoyment.

"Did you enjoy me?" Was Twinkle's only comment.

"You are without a doubt the love of my life" replied George.

A trillion light-years further than anyone can travel exists a planet controlled by benevolent Gods.

LIGHTENING

He had been traveling for such a long time in his spacecraft that he was becoming totally frustrated. To keep himself occupied. He had ranged far out in space to discover new worlds. Jules, for that, was his name had been gifted with a unique power through this gift could verify if it would be suitable for his kin to occupy that particular planet. His title was Space Ranger Prime. Eventually, he discovered a planet that would be acceptable to his people. Then having made that decision, he directed his spacecraft to descend to make a closer inspection. On landing, he realized that there was something very strange about the planet, it seemed to Jules to be antediluvian and very old-fashioned. This was further exemplified by some of the creatures that inhabited the planet. There was a terrible smell pervading the whole area, this was produced by huge hairy beasts that for the most part, seemed to be totally incontinent.

"Well, I have been to some shit planets on my travels, but this must take the crown for being the crappiest one"thought Jules

This was closely followed by his next thought" I better wake Cybil up"

Cybil was Jules's second in command and also his assistant, because of the long and tedious journey he had put her in hibernation. She was in fact a state-of-the-art artificial intelligence robot. Jules. pulled down a leaver and sent an electric shock coursing through her body, she woke up instantly and sat up.

"Hi boss this must be important, what would you like me to advise you on?"She said.

"I have just landed the ship on a planet, and I am not too sure of the inhabitants, will you analyse them for me?" requested Jules.

"Certainly" was Cybil's quick response.

Jules lounged back on the comfortable seat of the craft and waited for her reply, he knew. it would take a couple of hours before he received her response. He drifted into slumber mode while he waited for her response. He woke up with. a start to find that Cybil was standing over him.

"Well, I have performed my analysis, and I am not too certain about the results that I received, are totally banal," said Cybil.

"What do you mean by that?" demanded Jules.

"Yeah, for me it seemed almost impossible, but this planet is an electric conundrum. Those creatures have an offensive smell that is methane, which smells like rotten eggs. This is hardly surprising as"

The next instant there was a gigantic flash and forked lightning sizzled through the air and smashed into one of the hairy beasts that inhabited the planet, then it immediately defecated on the ground.

"As I was saying before, I was rudely interrupted, this planet is a seething mass of electricity that may strike at any time. However, we have just witnessed that the planet also protects its inhabitants, although struck by lightning the beast survived. In lightening, there must be a positive and negative charge to produce a huge burst of energy. The beast managed to dissipate the lightning strike by forming its own lightning conductor, so the strike passed straight through it." said Cybil.

Just then there was another lightning flash striking another hairy beast and confirming Cybil's theory.

"Do you know I am having second thoughts about this planet? My original instructions were to find a planet that would be safe for our burgeoning population. However., it now appears that the whole planet is fraught with danger, where our people could be struck by lightning at any time," said Jules.

"£Where then is your spirit of adventure?" replied Cybil.

"I don't think that is a very fair comment. I must make a judgment if it would be a safe world to land our people on. At this moment in time, it is certainly not," said Jules

"Look, you would have a problem if you selected this planet for our people to settle on, but it has spoken to me and has promised to cut down on the lightning activity,"said Cybil.

This is far above my comprehension of the situation that we are in, what do you mean by the planet has spoken to you?" inquired Jules.

Precisely what I said came back the instant response, somehow it invaded my mind said Cybil.

"That has to be a ridiculous comment. You are a state-of-the-art artificial intelligence robot, whereas I am a humanoid being. So please tell me why the superior electrical being that controls this planet should contact you Cybil, who is merely a robot," said Jules

"I have not the faintest idea"Cybil replied.

"If you are really. must know it was because I found her incredibly interesting" a loud voice thundered down from the skies above them

It then appeared that Jules had had an instant response from the omnipotent being. who lurked above them.

"You have been discussing the pros and cons of settling your humanoid people on my planet. Because of your predicament, I am prepared to grant you a couple of solid promises that will allow your people to settle comfortably on my planet. I confirm that there will be no sudden lightning storms and also will indulge in no illegal activities that would be detrimental to the health and well-being of the incoming humanoids" boomed out the voice from the sky.

"Well, I, must admit those stipulations seem to be very generous of you, but I will have to confer with my colleague concerning your offer" replied Jules.

"Then, I will await your reply" said the voice.

"By the way, what is your name? demanded Jules.

My name is very simple and consists of just three letters. My name is God" replied the voice. and vanished

"Yeah, I suppose that explains a great deal about our mythical being. We will just have to wait in fear and trepidation" continued Jules.

For the next few hours, they discussed whether or not the humanoid population should be settled on this planet that they had decided to call Hope. But still hadn't come up with a solution to their problem and time was running out.

Then to make everything even worse God returned.

"Have you made your final and binding decision? He bellowed out

"Unfortunately, we seem to be thoroughly indecisive in making a decision. Could you come back tomorrow? And we promise to give you an answer" beseeched Jules.

"Most definitely not I am God, and I am not in the habit of granting second chances. So, do as l, as I tell you or your lives will be forfeit" boomed out the God.

"Do you know, I have this suspicion that you are not a god at all, why do you swear and blaspheme all the time? Okay, you may be some minor entity sitting in your electrical cloud all day long bored out of your mind with nothing to do. So, what is your real name?" inquired Jules..

There seemed to be an electrical disturbance in the cloud. Perhaps he was thinking, how do I get out of this tricky situation? Eventually, a voice boomed out of the cloud

"My name is Fred, and you were correct in your assumption that I am not God. I have also decided to take a more level approach regarding our future negotiations"he said.

"Well, that is huge. change in direction as far as I am concerned and bearing this in mind, I will look favourably on settling our people on this planet" replied Jules

The negotiations that took place were long and fruitful and eventually, an agreement was concluded to transport the majority of humanoids on the planet by spaceship to planet Hope.

Fred was keeping his promise and the lightning strikes became few and far between. Both Jules and Cybil.had become incredibly busy preparing themselves for the incoming hordes of settlers. Jules was in constant communication with his home planet, who were now lining up spaceships for their final debarkation. Already plots of land had been marked. out for the housing of the incoming settlers. Everything was progressing swimmingly, which turned out to be the appropriate word ss the skies opened, and torrential rain poured down.

A frantic voice rang out from the clouds above.

"I thought that I was in control of the weather system, but it seems to have assumed its own control and there is nothing else that I can do," said the despairing voice of Fred

"Pull yourself together, it's only a dramatic inundation, you will encounter millions of settlers soon," said Jules.

A few months later the first settlers began to arrive, and then the hoards started to pour in.   The once-deserted planet became crammed with immigrants, which caused Fred to grumble incessantly. To aggravate matters even further Fred had lost control of the weather system. Whereas in the past he had control of lightning and the aftermath of thunder. Now it seemed that everything had become quite random. Both Juies and Cybil had just pushed their way through a throng of settlers when there was a terrific flash of lightning followed by an ominous rumble of thunder. It then transpired that the lightning had struck one of the huge hairy beasts but in the past, it had little effect This, time it struck the beast stone dead.

"This is a really bad situation that we are in, it seems that the parameters have been moved considerably. Whereas in the. past the, the beast would have survived by being earthed, that option seems to have been removed from the poor creature.

"That was totally uncalled for, everything seems to be changing in my world, this planet used to be a place of happiness and contentment," said Fred.

Both Jules and Cybil realized that Fred had decided to descend from his cloud and put in a personal appearance. He was absolutely huge and bright green and obviously was comfortable with his appearance.

"Well, good to meet you at last, you are really quite a scary individual," said Jules.

"You are, rather diminutive, with my stature I feel quite superior" replied Fred.

"Yeah, but they do say that the best things come in small packages" quipped Jules.

"Very amusing and quite trite, but then what are your ideas on climate change?" replied Fred.

"This is not purely a question of climate change, this is more about climate control, which of course functioned extremely well under your control, but now we have mayhem, so how do we cure the problem" demanded Jules.

"As you have pointed out it is entirely my problem and I will fix it" replied Fred.

This was followed by a gigantic flash and Fred disappeared.

"He is up to his magic tricks again" was Jules's sole comment

More ships landed and more disgruntled settlers made an appearance. In the clouds above the planet lightning, both forked and sheet danced among the clouds. Fred was obviously trying to regain control of the weather patterns. In the meantime, Jules and Cybil had retired to the relative safety of their ship

Cybil had been digesting vast amounts of information with robotic intensity

"Boss I can envisage a huge problem arising if Fred is unable to solve the problem of the weather system"sad Cybil

Having encountered Fred for the first time I have the utmost confidence in him to come up with a solution, after all, he has been sitting in his cloud for thousands of years with nothing more to do than twiddle his thumbs, then we arrived and gave him a new zest for life," said Jules.

Just then there was an explosion as, yet another hairy beast was struck by lightning and exploded.

They then received an urgent communication from their home planet, instructing them to make contact immediately, which they instantly did. The face of an angry Sirus Prime appeared on their screen.

"What in the blue blazes is happening on your planet? I have just witnessed a massive explosion as one of the strange hairy creatures exploded I guaranteed that it was a safe planet for the incoming settlers" grumbled Sirus.

"Well, if I told you wouldn't believe me anyway, suffice to inform you that we have a major problem," said Jules.

Then without further thought he shut down any further communication with Sirius Prime.

"Yeah, he didn't seem in a particularly good frame of mind and wouldn't have believed if you told him about a massive green god, so you had every right to terminate your communication," said Cybill

"You are very understanding for a robot, and I admire your discretion" replied Jules.

Unfortunately, Sirus Prime suffered from an inferiority complex and had delusions of grandeur. Therefore, when Jules shut down his viewing transmission without any explanation, he was a trifle miffed. Also, one of his ' worst vices was that he was totally bombastic and enjoyed humiliating minions on a regular basis. However, because of the uncertainty of the lightning strikes he had no intention of visiting the new planet as he had formulated a craven approach to it. Jules had an intense dislike of Sirus Prime as he had often witnessed his bullying tactics. Jules was not the kind of individual to harbour grudges and decided to approach Fred about his problem

."Did He also know of my existence?" Fred queried.

"No, most not. I had no reason to inform him of your existence" Jules replied.

". Are you accessible?" Jules shouted up at the cloud.

A few seconds later the massive green figure of Fred materialized in front of him. Fred then asked him a pertinent question.

"Do you respect Sirus Prime?"

"No, I detest and despise him" replied Jules

."Then I shall make him aware in a horrific manner that will teach him a short sharp lesson" responded Fred.

"Then if you want to put want to put the frighteners on him, it is perfectly okay with me" confirmed Jules

"Then, your wish is my command," said Fred and vanished.

Sirus Prime had radically changed his mind and had decided to visit Planet Hope to reprimand his representative on the planet Jules, for the rude way his communication had been terminated. Then, having landed on the planet and accompanied by four guards as he may have to arrest his dissident employee, he made his way over to the location where Jules's ship had been previously located. A strange creature blocked the way in front of them, it was extremely ugly and growled at them. Much to, the disquiet of the onlookers, it removed its head and hurled it at them. Tentacles then emerged from the body and blindly wavered towards them. Then both eyes of the dismembered head opened and glared toward them. Enough was enough and all of the guards including Sirus Prime, fled as if the hounds of hell were chasing them.

"Well, what did you think of my party piece?" Asked Fred.

He had just materialized beside Jules and Cybil, who were riveted to the screen in front of them.

"Hopefully, there will be .no more unannounced surprise visits from Sirus prime" replied Jules.

"I suppose. I that congratulations are in order, as you have seemed to have solved the weather problem. For example, we haven't had to experience random lightning strikes

"Yeah, it took a fair bit of tinkering, but I solved the problem and congratulations are in order" replied Fred

"That was really amazing how did you create all those terrible creatures and make them so horrific?" inquired Jules

"It was quite simple I created a video which was a clever mirage., that seemed to scare the wits out of Sirus Prime and his cohorts and had the desired effect that you wanted. However., this was purely a mesmerizing video with absolutely no physicality involved, nobody got hurt and it was interesting to see how fast Sirus Prime could run when he was terrified," said Fred.

"Yes, and the good thing about this scenario is I can't envisage the cowardly, Sirus Prime making a return visit here in quite a while" replied Fred

Then, something quite peculiar happened, whether it was one of Fred's clever mirages, neither Jules nor Cybil could be certain. Suddenly a magnificent white grand piano appeared and Fred seated himself at the piano and began to play. His performance was so dynamic, that lightning seemed to flash between his fingers and a tune began to emerge which was the Ride of the Valkyries. This was the fable of Viking warriors dying in battle and plunging into myth. Richard Wagner's music pounded out from the piano. Visions of immensely high mountains and deep ravines conjured up a picture of inhospitable terrain and misery. Then, Fred's tempo slowed down, and vast grassland and meadows spread before their eyes.

Both Jules and Cybil had found Fred's renditions most inebriating and had enjoyed his pianistic ability.

"Well, I took both of you on a journey through Norse mythology and hope that it met with your approval?" said Fred.

"Yeah, that was quite a journey. that you took us on, but I can only speak for myself, I found the whole experience incredible," said Jules

"Well, I know that being a robot my brain is wired completely differently from yours, however, I did find your musical, journey a complete blast" retorted Cybil.

.The complete demeanour of planet Hope seemed to be changing. Whereas in the past torrential rain and threatening thunderheads, had made everything seen as inhospitable. Now the skies were clear, and two suns beat down on the planet to herald yet another day.

Jules stood up and sauntered to the door of his spaceship.

"What is the program for the day boss?" Cybil demanded.

"We seem to have encountered a problem with a group of settlers, that should be sorted out" replied Jules.

"What is the problem?"Inquired Cybil

"This group of settlers complains of hearing strange voices that boom out of the air and which happens on a regular basis" replied Jules.

. He then continued"It's my job to sort it out"and advanced out of the door. When he returned, he went over to Cybil and gave her an account of his meeting with the group of settlers.

You wouldn't believe it Cybil, but these guys have only been here for a week and decided to indulge in some illegal brewing. They found some fungi with devilish properties, brewed the concoction with some herbs they found, and called it happy juice. It's no wonder they called it that I analysed it. and it is eighty percent proof of pure alcohol.   Then it is no wonder"that they are hearing strange voices as most of the time they are completely pissed and gone with the fairies," said Jules.

"That is the problem with all you humanoids, you test something out, and if it doesn't work, you walk away in another direction," said Fred

Jules went to the door of the spaceship and opened it, there standing in front of the door was the massive green figure of Fred.

"Oh, you have been up to your eves dropping snooping again?" said Jules.

"That comment is extremely unfair., those settlers you were meeting with, seemed to be shouting up at me to enable me to hear and I found your conversation intriguing, and by the way the fungi they were using is called Satan's kiss and is an aphrodisiac, although it is also loaded with alcohol," said Fred.

"Okay, I realize how interesting you find the humanoid race is and are beginning to feel rather patriarchal and have the best intentions. However, we would prefer to make our own decisions and not have our fate decided by some huge cloud hovering over us," said Jules.

"Yeah, I agree with you. The problems arise when I meddle with your affairs. Now I shall step back and review everything before I come to any decision," said Fred.

Then, having put his thoughts into words, he ascended back into the cloud.

"Well, we, and let's hope seemed to have established some kind of parameter. And let's hope that Fred abides by it," said Jules.

"Well, I think that we may have another problem to deal with before Fred abides by it," said Cybil.

"What exactly are you referring to?" Was Jules's immediate response.

"Alarmingly enough, I picked up on my monitor a huge shape heading towards us. which appears to be electrically charged," said Cybil.

"I suppose that wouldn't be Fred playing one of his funny tricks on us?" demanded Jules.

"No, there is a huge object within it and it seems to be spurting out blasts of energy at regular intervals," said Cybil.

"Do you know what you have just described?" it sounds to me that another spaceship is about to arrive, perhaps they are alien beings?" Replied Jules.

The next instant a massive spaceship passed over them and then landed next to them with pinpoint accuracy. Then the doors of the spaceship opened, and a huge green being descended.

"Would you believe it? the guy who had just descended on the hover bubble is an exact replica of Fred," said Jules.

"Perhaps, they are related in some way?" questioned. Cybil

"That Cybil is a distinct possibility. However, the guy who has just descended has a great deal, more gravitas about him than Fred.

"Do you mean that he has the appearance of being older?" asked Cybil.

"You are correct in your terminology" replied Jules.

"We seem to be receiving a visit from our large friend, he seems to be floating toward us on some kind of aerial device," said Cybil.

A few moments later the large green being was standing in front of the door of their spaceship. Jules went to the door of the spaceship and opened it.

"Greetings," said the large green being.

Jules came immediately to the point

"Pardon me for being so inquisitive, but there is an incredible likeness between yourself and another being, are you in any way related?" demanded Jules.

"Yes, we are indeed, and he is in fact our son. However, I better explain to you something that is called longevity. Fred as he calls himself was a very inquisitive child, although as a child he was an extraordinarily large one, he arrived on this planet over five thousand years ago. That is the problem with longevity because after a time everything becomes boring and banal. As far as I can remember I have existed for over fifty thousand years or maybe longer. The reason for my visit is to get acquainted with my son. By the way, I am called Sam" said the large green being

Then rather like his son, he vanished.

"Yeah, this seems to be getting weirder and weirder, I think that perhaps, the long levity may have scrambled his brains, maybe I shouldn't have said that as he could be listening in," said Jules.

"So, you have met my father, he is a crusty old curmudgeon and likes to pontificate on the good old days of twenty thousand years ago," said Fred.

"Yeah, and you are back to your previous bad habit of eavesdropping on everybody's conversations," said Jules.

"Yes, I realize that I made a. promise not to intervene unless there was a serious problem, well you have just encountered one in the shape of my father, you have no idea just how vindictive he can be," said Fred.

Both Jules and Cybil conferred with each other and decided that there was nothing more they could do. Obviously, Fred would approach his father and endeavour to arrive at a satisfactory conclusion for both.

"I fully understand the problem that he may have with his father on the technology side, over the thousands of years of separation between father and son. Fred was probably static in research and development, whereas his father streaked away. For example, the massive spaceship that he arrived in, performs gracefully and silently without any indication of its means of propulsion. That is scientific advancement beyond our wildest dreams, perhaps we can learn from it," said Jules

Nothing further seemed to be happening in the skies above them. Neither Fred nor Sam had made contact. Days turned into weeks and still, there was no contact, and the enormous spaceship still remained grounded. Then one night, there was a flash of lightning and a roll of thunder, and Fred stood in front of the spaceship door They then noticed that the huge spaceship, appertaining to, Fred's father, had disappeared

Then, there was a flash of lightning and the imposing figure of Fred appeared in front of their spaceship

"I realize now that I was instrumental in doing my father a terrible injustice, to my father. He visited me in my cloud, and we drank copious cups of lighting brew, which he adored, we got on famously and seemed to be a changed person and not the man that I once knew. It seemed that my mother had urged him to visit his long-lost son, which he did. He then informed me that although we have always considered ourselves immortal, in fact, we are not. Our scientists discovered that we are susceptible to a wasting disease known as old age rot. It now appears. That they may find a cure for this scourge, but we will have to wait and see," said Fred.

"Ok, then where does that leave you regarding the running of this planet?" Demanded Jules.

"Oh, didn't I tell you, he has no interest whatsoever in running such a primitive and backward planet," said Fred.

"Well, that comment your father made to all and sundry, wasn't very complimentary. perhaps he has an ulterior motive behind that comment?" replied Jules

"What are you inferring?" questioned Fred.

"Well, it is only a supposition that is probably untrue, but what if your father is jealous of his young son and is lurking in a cloud somewhere and planning to make a return visit," said Jules.

"What you are saying is complete nonsense and a load of baloney, my father gave me his word that he was leaving and never to return" replied Fred

"That is the interesting thing about super-human beings such as your father and yourself. My word is my bond. may have no relevance to him and may think that there is a non-moral excuse for everything that he does" retorted Jules.

Fred snorted in derision and vanished

A few hours later both Jules were still, engrossed in discussing all the vagaries of the situation that they had landed themselves in. They were still in deep discussion when the electrical storm smashed into them. Then on their screen, they saw something terrifying had appeared. It was a large shimmering object that crackled with electricity and was advancing towards them at hurricane speed. The object stopped and started hovering over them.

"What kind of creature is hanging over us" was Cybil's despairing question.

"I am not certain" was Jules's puzzled reply.

Then there was a buzzing sound, and a voice came out of the ether that surrounded them.

"I didn't mean to. Frighten you and I mean you no harm. The problem with me is that I am very young as I have only just been created. However, although I am a baby, I have been endowed with a name I am called Spark," said the creature.

"Well at least you have an identity, so where did you come from?" queried Jules.

The next instant there was a tremendous flash of lightning and the enormous green figure of Fred appeared.

"Hello Spark, good to see you" were Fred's only comments.

"How on earth do you know him?" Questioned Jules.

"The answer to that question is very simple, he is my son and my love child" replied Fred.

He then went on to explain that in the clouds above the planet Hope, numerous cloud people believed in free love. Amongst the cloud people was a beautiful maiden called Fire, they communed together. and fell passionately in love. The result. of our lovemaking was a baby boy that we called Spark," said Fred.

"Well, that is a delightful story of love and affection, and I must say your young son is superbly well-mannered.

Spark was hovering above them and seemed intent on catching the drift of their conversation. Although. He would occasionally swoop down as if to inspect some fictitious object. Fred had vanished obviously having been exhausted by the Continuing ritual.

"Yeah, that was a bit of an eye-opener. Who would have thought that there would be free love amongst these superior beings?"Said Jules.

"Yes, I am completely flummoxed, by the exploits of these supposed superbeings. I may be a robot but at least I have principles," said Cybil.

"Let me tell you, Cybil, you may be a robot, but you have a built-in system of something called common sense and that is functioning perfectly.

After their madcap few weeks, both Jules and Cybil were perfectly happy to let the world go by without incident. They did venture outside their spaceship on a couple of occasions to harvest the fungi' blazing heart, which they had acquired a passion for. They had just returned to their spaceship when the massive figure of Fred materialized in front of them blocking their entrance to the spaceship.

"Sorry for my uninvited appearance yet again, but we are about to encounter an exceedingly nasty situation," said Fred.

"Well, I was about to say how unusual, but that would have been a trite facetious" replied Jules

"Yeah. Then continuance of my description of the nasty situation. We have been invaded by a colony of ferocious creatures, that have the intention to occupy and terrorize all the inhabitants of planet Hope,"said Fred.

"Then what are we going to do about the defence of the planet?" demanded Jules.

"Absolutely nothing, it's not needed" replied Fred.

"What. do, you mean by it's not needed"asked a perplexed Jules.

"Well, I haven't been totally honest with you, although I correctly explained that these creatures were ferocious and predatory, they are also miniature, with traits of an ancestral heritage of Formicidae. Even a puny creature such as yourself with one giant step could wipe out the majority of them," said Fred.

"Thanks, a bundle., I don't really mind the insults you keep hurling at me, but I rarely receive a straight answer from you, and you keep leading me down the garden path"complained Jules.

"You have every right to complain, but why don't you go where the Formicidae are assembling and crush a few hundred of them" said a smirking Fred,

"Well at least that has cleared up the proposition of an alien invasion by horrific monsters," said Jules.

"Yes, they didn't sound very pleasant creatures" replied Cybil.

They had only just finished conversing, when there was a huge crash of thunder followed shortly after by a lightning strike.

"That is simply astounding, it's the wrong way round," said Jules.

"What exactly are you inferring by that? demanded Cybil.

"The peculiarity of this situation is that there was firstly a lightning strike closely followed by a crash of thunder. That is categorically the wrong way round," said Jules.

"Only, if. you believe it," said a voice.

"Who are you?" demanded Jules

"I am a time. lord but, you may call me Clock

Ok, Clock then will you explain? how the lightning struck before the thunder crashed"inquired Jules.

"Yes, of course, I can, and if you pardon the pun. It is all a matter of timing," said Clock.

"Then, are you able? To adjust the time sequence between the lightning strike and the crash thunder" inquired Jules.

"Of course, I can I am a time lord. I will reverse the sequence, and consider it reversed,"said Clock.

Then, almost immediately, there was a flash of lightning followed by a crash of thunder.

"Success, he's changed it, we are in sequence again," said Cybil.

"Well, I will be off then as I have a multitude of things to do. Let me know if you have any more problems with time and I will see what I can do?" said Clock

A few more days rushed over the horizon and a huge bellow announced the arrival of Fred. He was standing in front of their spaceship blocking the door with his huge frame

"I am just checking on how my closest friends are faring as I haven't heard from them in quite a few days," said Fred.

"Yeah, we have had quite an exciting time over the past few days and met an interesting character," said Jules.

"Elaborate" was Fred's swift reply.

"Well, we met this guy who said he was a time lord and had the power to control time. His name was Clock. The problem was, and this may interest you, the thunder was arriving before the lightning," said Jules

"That really is incredibly strange. and really interests me because of the weather connotations, so what happened next?" Said, Fred.

"Well, he had stated that he was a time lord, but I had no idea what he was talking about" replied Jules.

"Go on, I hope that you will offer me a rapid conclusion and not keep me hanging in suspense for eternity,"said Fred.

"Yeah. The unbelievable happened and somehow, he reversed time and corrected the order of the lightning and thunder," said Jules.

"This time lord geezer has the power to control time, he sounds like somebody worth knowing, how do I get in touch?" demanded Fred.

"That may be quite difficult as he said that if you have any problems let me know what I can do?" said Jules

"Then, it sounds to me that you have no direct way to contact him," said Fred.

"Maybe, there is a way to contact him, is after he is all a time lord. Perhaps if I shout loud enough, he will hear me" said Jules.

"Don't be ridiculous, he can't possibly hear you," said Fred

"Well, that is a strange comment coming from a huge green monster, who has the mistaken idea that he is superior to everyone", said a voice.

"Where, by the nine rings of strontium did that voice come from?" demanded Fred.

"That seems incredible, but I think that I might have just contacted the time lord" replied Jules.

"Then, If that is the case I take it all back you have not been ridiculous in shouting out, he obviously heard you," said Fred.

"Well, as introductions are imperative, I will put on an appearance," said Clock

Then after waiting for a lengthy period of time,. Without witnessing an appearance, Fred exclaimed. I can't see you?"

"That is. Hardly surprising, I am a time lord and invisible" was Clock's reply

"Do you know, you are exactly the kind of individual that I would love to meet and you have the added quality of b being invisible, said Fred.

"Ok, I hear what you say and it makes me cringe because I am not only invisible but a time lord that is able to alter time, you are under the false impression that we would make a great team to conduct nefarious activities. However, unfortunately, for you, I have no intention of betraying my trust as a time lord whatever the inducement may be" said Clock

"I applaud your honesty," said Jules.

"Stay out of this conversation puny one as it is no concern to you," shouted Fred.

"Your introduction to me of this green monster was a bad mistake but I bear you no ill will and am off on my travels again as I have a myriad of things to do. Farewell" said Clock

"What are you doing?"Asked Cybil.

"I am daydreaming"was Jules's reply

"What does daydreaming entail?" was Cybil's next question

"Picture this I, am drifting through space with no particular place to go. Then suddenly in my dream, a beautiful image appears of a bright red heart flower. This, however, is no ordinary flower and possesses extraordinary powers for example, if you were to breathe in its intoxicating fragrance, it instantly transforms your outlook on life, doubts and the cares of the world would vanish, to be replaced by joy and happiness," said Jules.

"This flower sounds wonderful, where can I obtain it from?" asked Cybil

"It is impossible to obtain as it is only in my dream" Jules replied.

Then outside their spaceship, they heard a loud bang that vibrated the whole ship. Then there was an ominous silence

"That was probably Fred involving himself in some kind of crazy experiment," said Jules

Then there was a heavy hammering on the door of their spaceship

"I heard that" roared out the irate voice of Fred.

"Of course, you did" murmured Jules.

When he arrived at the door of the spaceship and opened it, there was Fred lounging in the huge chair that he had constructed for himself a couple of days ago.

"Good to see you again, and what an interesting creature the time lord, unfortunately, he sussed me out almost immediately as a partnership we could have done great things together. It's my opinion that he is far too honest for his own good" chortled Fred

"Anyway, I have a project that. You may wish to be involved with, no doubt you remember my father and his enormous faster-than-light ship, well, He gave me some advice and pointed me in the right direction," said Fred

"What exactly do you mean by that?" queried Jules.

"My father gave me the necessary information to build and fly an FTL spaceship which was powered by nuclear fusion and granted unlimited energy to the spaceship. However, I encountered a further problem with the venture, having secured a power source still needed an incredibly hard material to fabricate the spaceship," said Fred

"Then how did you overcome?" that problem inquired Jules.

"Quite a simple answer I used gravity" Fred replied

"Yeah, now it seems to me that it is getting a little bit far-fetched. How does gravity work?" said Jules.

"Well, gravity possesses intense pulling power and planet Hope has two moons which means that its pulling power is increased exponentially. This has the effect of creating exceedingly hard substances on Planet Hope. These substances I was able to utilize to strengthen the complete structure of my FTLship," said Fred.

"Then I suppose that my obvious question must be, what do you need me along for? when you have already sorted out all the pertinent points of your epic journey" questioned Jules.

"There is a simple answer to this question, I enjoy your company, and if we start, it will be a long and hazardous trip" replied Fred.

"Well thanks for the offer and I will think about it," said Jules.

"When are you thinking of leaving?? Jules added

"Yeah, I have a multitude of people of people say goodbye to and it may take a couple of months," said Fred.

Out in the furthest reaches of space, over twenty billion light-years from planet Earth is a planet called Hope, which is still waiting for the lightning god, Fred to return.

BOAR CONSTRICTOR

There seemed to be a serious problem with his breathing, but he couldn't find the problem, he had drifted through space for millenniums and was increasingly tired of his everlasting journey. A thought lurched into his feverish brain and told him to self-replicate, which he did and immediately felt better. He cast his mind back in time and all he remembered was a vast explosion and the planet he was on being split asunder. He felt cramped and confined in his eternal prison and longed for release. He stretched languorously although he still felt inhibited and wanted to break out of his prison. Yet every second he became more sentient and became more aware. Then as his brooding continued, there was a shuddering motion to his craft and it came to an abrupt halt However, he felt incredibly languorous and stretched himself into an enormous position, it was only then that he realized that he was gargantuan. It was then that something extraordinary started happening to him. He felt a need to shed his skin. He stretched out until he could go no further. And felt a rippling along his whole body. He then stretched even further and slid out of his old skin, having completed this operation he felt totally energized. Overhead the planet wherever he was, shone a huge yellow moon, which was no threat to his well-being. Then suddenly, as if somebody had switched the light on, night became day. Replacing the moon, glared down a huge red burning sun, which had an instant. Effect on Boa, which he had decided to call himself. The glaring heat flowed down on him, and he felt wonderful. Having glanced in the direction of his space conveyance, he began to realize that his mode of conveyance was very primitive, to say the least. Boa had been blasted into space on nothing more than a huge rock, it was no wonder that he had trouble breathing. Boa then looked around him to verify if there were any signs of life on this planet, it didn't appear that there was. Somehow through. His psyche, he had felt the need to procreate, he didn't. Know what entailed but doubt he would find out

"Well, we have been traveling. companions that I thought I should make acquaintance with when our rock was split asunder and hurtled into space, I was part of our explosive exit, by the way, my name is Nina.

"This is incredible and just when I was thinking about procreating," said Boa

"Then what exactly does procreating mean?" demanded Nina.

"I haven't a clue, but there is no doubt we will have fun finding out" replied Boa.

"However, we have a serious problem in establishing where we are, we seem to be on a planet where the concept of night and day exists. The night-time. is cool and pleasant, whereas the days are ferociously hot," said Boa.

Yeah, I wouldn't like to stay in the sun for too long, it was blisteringly and far too hot" Nina retorted.

"Do you think that? there could be other space travellers on this planet, perhaps with not such benign intentions as us" Nina continued.

"These creatures, whatever they may be, I wouldn't be afraid of in the slightest," said Boa.

Then having proclaimed that, Boa stretched himself drew himself up to his gargantuan size, and opened his enormous mouth.

"Besides this, I have made a vow to protect my lady love Nina from any foul creature that she may encounter," said Boa.

Nina turned towards her avowed. Protector, who was truly magnificent in his grandeur, also felt a twinge of passion toward him.

"Ok, in the spirit of true adventure, shall we investigate what appears to be our new home?" said Boa.

Under, the cool protection of the huge yellow moon, they set out on their journey of discovery. Progress was slow as they encountered many weird and wonderful things on their journey. Massive trees and palms towered above them as they progressed further into the planet. Amazingly multi-coloured flowers. With exotic perfumes, embroidered on their journey. Then the sun came out with all its ravening intensity that indevoured to boil anything that lay in its war. Both waited in the shade of the mighty trees until the moon cast its cool shadow and nighttime descended.

"Thank goodness. For nighttime arriving, the sun is totally stifling. Mind you I was beginning to feel quite drowsy from the effect of those heady perfumes emitting from those exotic plants,"said Nina.

"Ok, I catch your drift but to escape from that searing sun was a great relief," said Boa

There was no culmination to their exploration as both felt an insatiable drive to continue ever forward. Nina and Boa were finding their journey incredibly exciting as their exploration progressed even further. Boa was amazed by the energy and enthusiasm that exploded from Nina's with every movement that she made. However, they still hadn't encountered any sentient creatures on their continuing quest. Boa was dumbfounded by Nina's energy levels, where does it come from? he kept asking himself, she is only half my size.

"Well, we meet at last another sentient being I am really pleased to make your acquaintance,"said a voice.

"Yeah, we have been searching for another sentient being. Having said that where are you? You seem to be invisible"demanded Boa.

"Well, I can see you perfectly well and from up here, you, look horrific," said the voice.

Thanks for the compliment, but I still can't see you, show yourself" requested Boa.

The next, instant a strange and grotesque creature appeared out of the trees ahead of them, it had a vulture's head and the body of a crow. And this ungainly creature crashed into the ground ahead of them,

"What exactly are you? I have to say you look horrific yourself" exclaimed Boa

."Yes, I am not as beautiful as I would like to be and was created from a jumble of atoms, but you call me Sam," said the voice

"Ok, then Sam is your sobriquet from now on" chimed in Nna

"Where did that voice come from? Oh, you are a smaller version of him," said Sam.

Then what kind of creatures are both of you?" queried Sam.

"Both of us are Boa constrictors and we have the nasty habit of encircling and crushing our victims to death," said Boa.

Sam made a point of backing away from them.

"You know I don't think that you are very pleasant people, and I will endeavour to o stay away from you," said Sam.

At this repost, Boa roared with laughter..

"There is really no need to fear us, we promise to do you no harm and let that be an end to your anxiety"Boa replied.

"In that case, I am satisfied with your honest response and would be delighted to accompany you on your perilous journey" replied Sam.

With that response, the three of them continued their journey, The strange creature, who was a jumble of atoms, turned out to be quite useful, he was their spy on the sky. and also, an early warning system, He fluttered down and crashed into the ground, he obviously hadn't mastered the art of a graceful landing. However, his report. Was quite alarming.

"Just ahead of us over the rise, there seems to be a pitched battle taking place, it was very difficult to see who the combatants were I was too high up" reported Sam.

Sam took to the sky again and began to hover over where the battle was ensuing. Then both went to the top of the ridge and gazed down at the frenzied battle that was taking place. Both Goa and Nina remembered that Sam had found that as he was so high up it was hard to distinguish the combatants, both now realized why. there may have been a couple of hundred of them, but they were minute.

"Well, that explains the whole scenario that is taking place. Visually these tiny creatures seem to have inherited the same jumble of atoms as our spy-in-the-sky friend," said Boa.

"I agree with you, except our friend doesn't seem to have inherited the bellicose nature of these miniature warriors" replied Nina.

Then there was a loud squark and thudding into the earth which heralded the arrival of Sam

"I am sorry about that I seem to have blotted my copybook. Whatever, a copybook is?" Said Sam.

"It appears, that I completely misled you on the stature of these tiny people and for that, I apologize," said Sam.

"Well, I suggest that we plan our next move must be to investigate this planet of mystery," said Boa

Sam, as soon as he heard this comment immediately perked up and flew up to retain his customary position of spy in the sky.

"What are we going to do about the little creatures who insist on knocking the shit out of each other?" Asked Nina.

"I have no problem. With that, they are so minute that if we were attacked it would be like being hit with feather dusters" Goa replied.

Sam swooped in and landed with his customary crash, shooting huge clouds of dust into the air.

"I have been flying around for ages and have nothing to report, so I thought that I would pass the time away by having a chat," said Sam.

"That really is a crazy idea, you are our spy in the sky, and without your operational skills, we will be as blind as a bat, so elevate yourself and scan the far horizons" beseeched Goa.

Not wishing to incur the wrath of the huge serpent, Sam quickly sped into the upper atmosphere and disappeared. Both had been encased in dense forests from which they emerged. Ahead of them lay mile after mile of grassland that went on forever, there was still no sigh no sign of their early warning system. Nina had admonished Boa for the unfortunate way that he treated Sam.

"He's not your servant or slave, treat him with more respect," she said.

When Sam did arrive back, he made them aware of his presence by landing on an area of grassland that cushioned his landing, he seemed to be visibly shocked and was shaking.

"You look absolutely petrified about what has happened to you." Boa demanded.

"These creatures are enormous almost the same size as you. They have this terrible stench that permeates everywhere. I have this awful feeling that they may be cannibalistic," said Sam..

"What makes you think that they are cannibals?" queried Nina.

"On my mission, I got close enough to view their inner sanctum and it was quite was. Also, a huge caldron in the centre of the inner sanctum. Every now and then one of these gross creatures would take a wooden paddle-like object into the caldron and give it a violent stir. I am certain. That these creatures eating their own kind" gasped out Sam.

"Then, can you give us a more accurate picture of what these monsters look like Sam?" said Boa.

"Well if you want an accurate description of these monsters, I will have to say that they are mostly grotesque and look like a larger version of myself" replied Sam.

"Then there we have the answer, you have already stated that you are merely a jumble of atoms These creatures are in exactly the same mould but a far larger batch, these grotesque creatures as you so aptly put it, may even be your relatives," said a smiling Boa.

"Whatever, you say I am not a cannibal," said an angry Sam.

"You most definitely are not, but there again it is quite possible that those creatures cannot be tarred with the same brush," said Boa.

What do you horrific. There was a multitude of skulls and skeletons and dismembered body parts that lay scattered across the ground. There mean by that?" queried Sam,

"To put it simply they may not be cannibals and have an adequate explanation for all those anomalies" replied Boa.

"OK, then what are we proposing to do next"? inquired Sam.

"We are going to investigate and not procrastinate" replied Boa...

"Yeah, we intend to visit your so-called relatives and discover exactly what their intentions are. and take the necessary action if so needed" continued Boa.

Then having made this decision, they set off in the direction of the inner sanctum. Sam. Had resumed his previous position and was acting as the spy in the sky to warn of any incoming danger. It was over a two-hour journey to get to the inner sanctum and Nina found the journey both laborious and boring but nevertheless carried on regardless. Sam kept popping on back at frequent intervals to furnish them with further information, most of which was spurious. Nighttime fell a couple of times on their journey to be relieved of its duty by the searing heat of the sun. Eventually, they arrived. at their destination, just as nighttime had fallen and it was pitch black. Sam descended and they parked themselves until dawn by the entrance of the cave that led to the inner sanctum.

The daytime cycle resumed its responsibility, with its customary temperature of searing heat. Boa had learned one thing about his powers and had discovered that he possessed the power of hypnosis. Guarding the entrance to, the inner sanctum was a huge creature that endeavoured to bar his way. However, he was no match for the gigantic serpent who transfixed him with a basilisk stare. Then the three of them passed the hypnotized guard and entered the inner sanctum. The cavern was enormous and stretched into the far distance. In the middle of the chamber was one of Sam's supposed relatives who was stirring a huge caldron. The creature. Seemed to be enjoying this culinary experience and was singing loudly to himself. Every now and then he would break something in half and throw it into the pot Boa slithered forward to enable himself to obtain a clearer view of the cooking process. The chef grabbed a large handful of something and dropped it into the pot. Immediately a blue flame flared up and then expunged itself. Boa edged forward and breathed in the vapours that were exuding from the cauldron. He then realized that something was not quite right. A few days ago. Sam had scorched himself very badly whilst trying to light a fire, the same smell that had emanated from Sam now invaded all three of their minds.

"I owe you an apology, Sam, It now appears that you were correct in your original supposition of this race being cannibals," said Boa.

"Well, now that you have uncovered the dreadful truth, what do you intend to do about it?" demanded Sam.

"Yes, we seem to have encountered a huge problem, having said that it is there to be solved," said Nina.

"Well, we obviously have to change their tastes by some means or other. Perhaps we could offer them cookery classes" postulated a smirking Sam.

"That was not in the slightest a helpful, comment, from the creature who made this dire discovery in the first place" replied Boa.

"However, I probably have the means to make certain that this dreadful occurrence never happens again. If we can arrange for all four hundred of these cannibals to attend a meeting at the same time, I may be able to hypnotize these creatures to see an error in their ways" continued Boa.

"Once before witnessed the chamber was full to bursting. At the entrance of the cave is a huge gong, one of the elders of the community struck it several times, and a short time later the chamber was packed to the rafters" replied Sam.

"Then that is exactly the format we shall use to enable mass hypnotism to take place. Sam, you may have the honour of striking the gong. Then in a couple of hours' time, the creatures should start to assemble," said Boa.

Then added "And let the party begin"

As instructed by his mentor Sam struck the gong, whilst a hypnotized guard was oblivious to any movement he made. Then gradually the creatures with cannibalistic tendencies began to filter through. In the meantime, Boa had made his. own a

"Do you know Sam; we may have discouraged them from continuing this hideous practice we will djustments to the mirrors that adorned the surrounding walls. Now all the mirrors were focused on the largest mirror which would be crucial to Boa's hypnotic powers of persuasion. Eventually, the vast cavern became crammed with cannibalistic creatures most of whom seemed to be indulging in intense arguments with each other. Now, estimating that the time was right Boa took control of the whole operation. There was a blinding flash that emanated from the largest mirror, which caught the attention of the majority of the creatures. Then the cold hypnotic. Eyes of the Great Serpent known as Boa appeared in the mirror and his audience was immediately transfixed. He then lectured his captive audience on the evils of eating your brothers and sisters. Whereas before the audience had been garrulous and inattentive, they hung on his every word. Again and again, he repeated the mantra. Cannibalistic tendencies are evil. Now a silence ensued, to be replaced. by animated conversation. have to wait and see." said Boa.

"Well, I can honestly say that you held them in the palm of your hand, you were magnificent," said Nina.

"Yes, I was rather superb, wasn't I? remarked a boastful Boa.

Then, they waited to hear the result of the meeting, the main topic being to ban cannibalism. Eventually, they were. Informed by the spy in the sky that the meeting was to be held that day. The three of them arrived early the next day to hear the verdict. One of the elders. stood on one of the benches and asked a direct question.

"I am not certain how this has happened, but we were always happy if a relative died, even a small child, to eat them,"said the elder.

"You are so wrong in your assumption, that you should eat are brothers and sisters, in the past, some of us have eaten plague victims, and what happened? They all contracted the plague and died"said a voice in the crowd.

"Yes, I do admit that was an unfortunate outcome. However, there is nothing better to eat than a fresh young child covered in delicious gravy" said the elder.

"You seem to have a major flaw in your appetite, and it is terribly wrong what you stand for," said the voice of the crowd

"You sir are impertinent and a blaggard. Officer. Arrest that man"

No sooner had he screamed out this instruction than an arrow flew out of the crowd and buried itself in the scrawny chest of the elder who pitched forward and died.

"What in the blue blazes is happening" moaned a bewildered Sam. who was secreted in an alcove near his companions.

"It appears that not everyone agrees with cannibalistic tendencies and therefore resorted to violence as retribution" replied Boa.

"I am certain that your hypnotic endeavours must have swayed the majority to vote against the disgusting custom of cannibalism," said Nina.

Although the guards had been very thorough in their search for the rogue archer, they had failed to arrest him, and he had disappeared back into the crowd. The gong sounded again, and the crowd fell into an uneasy silence. A tall figure appeared on the rostrum and stood there whilst commanding silence.

"A vote has been taken and has been confirmed and passed by a unanimous electorate. From this day hence, it shall be illegal to indulge in the evil practice of cannibalism which is now the law and cannot be broken" said the man on the rostrum.

"Weii, we seemed to have obtained our ultimate objective, that of outlawing the hideous practice of cannibalism. I suppose that some kind of celebration would be in order," said Boa.

"Then if a celebration.is in the offing I know exactly what I would like to do," said Nina

"Then, don't keep me in suspense, what would you like to do?" replied Boa.

"Hold me in your coils and love me" was Nina's quick reply.

Their lovemaking was intense and pleasurable. Goa held her in his coils and crushed her to him and they didn't emerge from their place of intercourse for a couple of months. When they did finally emerge, they were both totally exhausted.

"That was quite amazing and the contortions that you performed put me in a dreamlike trance. I felt that I could go on forever and never release my hold," said Nina.

The serpent. Niña led a long and happy life and with Boa sired many children.

On a planet, a billion light-years from Earth lived creatures who believed in fairness and equality ad infinitum.

ORIGINAL WORLDS BOOK TWO

BUBBLES AND ATMOSPHERE

He existed, but wasn't certain why? Then where was he? Again, there seemed to be no answer to the question.?. He focused his mind if indeed he possessed one, and concentrated. He seemed to be floating through a wispy haze that constantly shifted in another direction. A beam of bright light pierced his traveling mode and illuminated the region that surrounded him. A huge. object appeared in front of him, and without realizing it he encountered his first planet. The next instant. He seemed to be dragged in the direction of the planet and there could be no release from his binding to the planet. However, he discovered that somehow, he was able to analyze the constituent of the cloud that masked the planet. First, he discovered that one of the main makeup of the cloud was something called oxygen another major constituent of the cloud was something known as hydrogen. There were many other constituents of the. cloud a red warning sign warned him that it was toxic All the time he was building up his knowledge of his environment. He had already deduced that the cloud that enveloped the planet was in fact the planet's atmosphere. As he seemed to be in no way constrained, he decided to investigate the planet further, in the back of his brain was a knowledge that perhaps there are creatures inhabiting his planet. With. With this thought in mind, he hurled himself through the protective atmosphere and into the unknown. Then when he arrived on the planet, he gazed in wonder at his surroundings. He seemed to be seated in a lofty position, perhaps on a high mountain, although incredibly enough, these new words seemed to magically appear in his mind…

Then, beyond this, a new vision danced before his. eyes. It seemed to be a vast stretch of a blue-green colour that stretched on for miles. However, in this instance, he knew immediately what it consisted of. It was a combination. of two of the major constituents that made up the planet Both hydrogen and oxygen were involved in combining to produce something that was called water. As he peered down from his lofty perch, Atmos that was wat he had decided to call himself. He found himself captivated by the twinkling waters that surrounded him. He realized that there were many occurrences that were happening that he didn't fully understand. When the huge red orb appeared from nowhere and proceeded to hover above the planet, he was even more confused. The red orb also seemed to be having a dramatic effect on Atmos. The heat that. poured down from the red orb had the effect of forming vast clouds of impenetrable fog that confused Atmos even more. It was quite weird how it was affecting him, as he was very aware that he was still part of the composition of the planet. Then something turned the light off and the red orb vanished. Without realizing day had turned into night. Atmos realized that his cloud of gasses covered the planet and was somehow important to the protection of this unknown world. He decided to investigate the composition of the planet. He found that through a process of experimentation, he was able to detach himself and float independently in a bubble-like mode of transport. He floated down and gracefully landed on a strange material. His bubble allowed him the flexibility to stretch out in virtually all directions. The material that had landed on was hard and uncompromising, it was also extremely hot. Without realizing his predicament, he landed on a mini volcano. However, the bubble allowed him protection and insulated him against heat. Atmos was uncertain of what his next move should be when it was entirely taken out of his hands.

"I am not too certain where I am, but I must be somewhere. I am called Bubbles" the voice said.

"Splendid to meet you Bubbles but where exactly are you? Queried Atmos.

"That is a very pertinent question and easy to answer, I am inside you" replied Bubbles

Atmos was completely flummoxed by this remark, but then by concentrating extremely hard, he realized that he and the unknown voice were seated alongside each other in the bubble conveyance. The amazing. thing- about this synergy was that they both seemed to have separate thought processes

"This is quite bizarre, both of us share the same thoughts and yet we will have to come to a joint decision," said Atmos.

"This may not be as difficult as you may think we are able to have an internal discussion on this" replied Bubbles.

"Ok a fair comment, but what if we both disagree on an important matter" replied Atmos.

"That will be easy enough, I will agree to disagree" replied Bubbles

"Yeah, but that is hardly the point, you have already stated that whatever I want you will accept, that is hardly fair on you,"said Atmos

"Maybe not but I will survive,"said Bubbles.

They both exited from their conveyance and one gazed at their surroundings and exclaimed in unison that there seemed to be no end to the blue-green vision.

Bubbles, then seemed to stop in mid. Thought.

"I know exactly what this is, it suddenly explained itself by appearing in my mind it is an ocean,"said Bubbles.

"Then, how can you explain the fact? that although we share the same mind, I received no notification that it was an ocean" complained Atmos.

"Then, it seems pretty obvious.to me, that somehow are shared mind is possibly being diverted. Perhaps there is a superior being out there that is controlling our thought patterns and will only release only thoughts that are not detrimental t its own thought patterns" suggested Bubbles.

"That really is. a spurious suggestion and I can't envisage any likelihood in it being the true scenario,"said Atmos.

"Well, anyway having a chance to explore that greater unknown known as the ocean," said Bubbles.

They ventured down to the edge of the blue-green ocean and hesitatingly climbed down into the ocean; both their minds seemed to be locked into a lover's embrace. However, what happened next was completely unexpected, as he approached the ocean they descended by a rocky path until eventually, they walked into the ocean. They had no idea of what the ocean consisted of and carried on walking, it seemed to be A vest' flat plain that continued forever.

"Do you know, there is something exceedingly strange about, this so-called ocean? I am attuned to the atmosphere of this planet and have decided that we should be walking across something called water., except if it were water we would sink or drown"said Atmos"

"Do you think that you have made a mistake and your supposition has led you in the wrong direction" replied Bubbles

"No, I firmly believe that my judgment is totally correct and this area that are walking across should be water," said Atmos.

"Then I will bow to your superior judgment, but why aren't we sinking orb swimming" retorted Bubbles.

"Well, we could continue to explore further and find out" replied Atmos.

The duo explored further and continued to walk across the water. Then, after about half an hour of trudging to the far horizon at the instigation of Bubbles, they halted

"This water that we are traversing, is immeasurably cold. I think that it is probably something that is called ice,"said Bubbles.

"Yeah, you could be correct in your assumption, and it certainly explains how we are not swimming and or drowning, but to do that there must have been a huge drop in temperature to enable this world to freeze over" replied Atmos.

"With such inhospitable temperatures as these, it is entirely possible that there are no creatures on this planet as all may have perished" replied Bubbles.

However, no sooner had he come to that conclusion than there was a mighty crash, and a huge monster smashed through the surface ice. This was a truly terrifying creature with Avast's mouth agape, that hadn't eaten for a thousand years. It had somehow sensed the duo and sliced its way through the ice pack in its endeavour to reach them. But unfortunately. For the behemoth, it was to no avail, and he failed to reach his intended prey.

"That was quite a scary moment, it seemed intent on gobbling us up," said Bubbles

"Well, we all have our individual problems, but we learn to get over them," said a voice

"Where did that voice come from?" questioned a perplexed Atmos.

"It derived from me,"said the huge monster

"This is very weird a few minutes ago you were endeavouring to devour us and yet now we have a talking monster, explain why,"said Atmos

"It is very simple really, became extremely bored. I was stuck in this vast expanse of absolutely nothing where something never happens, and I spotted the two of you and needing a bit of excitement I decided to scare you rigid,"said the monster

"You have been totally misled as there is only one of us although we do exist in the same body" replied Atmos.

The monster appeared to be bemused and confused.

"Then you are telling me that although you are the same person you have different thought processes. I. find that quite incredible and beyond belief, by the way as you both have names you may call me Slicer," said the monster.

"Well, I have a perfect understanding of why you wish to be called Slicer. It's those huge teeth that you are adorned with, that are terrifyingly appropriate," said Atmos.

A voice then entered his mind saying do you trust him? His reply was instant

"Would you trust him with a name like that? he is the stuff of nightmares a bad dream with nowhere to go"replied Atmos.

Bubbles then digested his reply and thought for a moment before responding

"Yeah, I totally understand why you have misgivings about this fellow but is it fair to judge somebody purely on the name that they have adopted?" Bubbles replied.

"Well, in this case, it is. Probably incorrect that you can't judge a book by its cover, turn away for a moment and he will devour you," said Atmos.

It was then the massive creature turned its ponderous head towards its previously intended victims.

"I would be most grateful if you could turn up the volume in your voices, I am unable to grasp the content of your conversation," he said in a sneering voice.

"It sounds to me as if you are suspicious of our intentions" Atmos bellowed out.

"Not at all, I am fully aware that you are both if use your e-collective title week feeble creatures and are no threat to me in the slightest. Whereas I am the stuff of nightmares with every intention of a dismembering limb from limb," said Slicer

There was a moment of silence before Atmos whispered s furtive response.

"Hopefully, if I speak in a subdued voice, he will not be able to hear me. We have a huge advantage. over this Neanderthal creature, we are two, and yet the power of our minds registers us as one. With our supreme intelligence, we should be able to run rings around this moron," said Atmos.

An extremely loud voice thundered out behind them.

"Speak up why are you whispering, if you think that you are able to outwit me, it will turn out to be your most unpleasant experience" threatened Slicer.

"Why are you so suspicious of our intentions? You have stated that we are weak and feeble creatures and so what can you possibly fear from us?" replied Bubbles.

"You are right what have I to fear from such insignificant creatures as you" retorted Slicer.

"Thereby lies this monster's problem, he suffers from vanity. We in our duopoly mode will be able to use this to destroy him. He is under the impression that he is indestructible and firmly believes that he is able to obtain all that he wishes, we shall use this against him," said Atmos.

"You. are indeed a fearsome creature and very few creatures can stand in your way, except perhaps on the Ice Giant," said Atmos.

"Where is this Ice Giant to be found? I will rend him limb from limb" roared Slicer.

"He is standing just behind you, waiting to exterminate you". replied Atmos.

Slicer immediately turned round and glared at the huge ice mountain behind him. The reflection of the ice mountain danced before Slicer's eyes and gave him the impression that a vast white creature was striding toward him. In his crazed mind, he charged at the Ice Giant knowing that his defeat would not be acceptableHoe.However, with his unstable vision, Slicer smashed into the mighty Ice Giant bringing huge chunks of ice raining down on him. Finally, with a splintering crash, the ice mountain collapsed on top of SlicerSplintering him into small pieces.

"Well, that was interesting, so what do we do now as our nemesis has gone"? inquired Bubbles.

"Yeah, I think that perhaps for a short while, we sit on our haunches and wait for our joint mind to clear" suggested Atmos.

"However, we have a huge planet to explore, and we are sure to discover many exciting things in our journey of discovery." continued Athos.

It was then that the intrepid explorers continued their journey. Then after a great deal of time, as they strode through the landscape, the scenery began to change. The icefields were replaced by rocky outcrops and eventually vast meadowlands that were garlanded with hosts of brightly covered flowers. Occasionally, on their travels, they ceased their journey to take in the amazing colorful landscapes spreading out before them. In the far distance, there were huge animals that were indistinct in their movements. In the sky above them, flew enormous reptilian birds that gave out harsh menacing cries. Eventually, they halted their journey and seated themselves amidst the brightly coloured flowers in one of the meadows.

"We really have covered a vast distance and the perfume from these flowers is quite intoxicating, I am beginning to feel quite drowsy," said Bubbles.

It was just then, that a huge bird that had been hovering over them, landed with a warning squark.

"You are lying right in the centre of a group of flowers that we call the death flowers. These flowers have the propensity to expunge a powerful narcotic from which the sleeper never wakes up and sleeps forever," said the bird.

"Then thanks for the warning, have you a name that we can call you by?" said Atmos.

"Well, I am known to all my friends as Alarm, I can't think why," said the bird. And flew off.

"We seemed to be entertained all the time wherever we go," said Bubbles.

"Yes, wherever we are the epitome of laughter and high jinks, I am not certain if it is a good or a bad thing.?" postulated Atmos.

Bubbles made no reply to this conundrum and remained silent.

From then on Atmos was determined to explore the whole region, regardless of the danger that it would entail. Both Atmos and Bubbles were soon in their stride as they trudged over enormous distances. Then on the horizon, they spotted a huge bird that hurtled toward them forcing them to duck. It then transpired that their attacker was nonother than Alarm who found the whole incident very amusing.

Atmos shouted up at the sky where the disappearing bird was now just a twinkle in the sky.

"That wasn't amusing in the slightest, luckily, I didn't have a drink as I might have spilled it"he shouted out.

Bubbles, however, had found the situation extremely amusing and couldn't stop chortling.

The courageous duo carried on their exploration at a prodigious rate and night turned into day on several occasions. As temperature, whether cold or hot had little effect on them, they slept in the open under the twinkling stars. They also had another advantage over other creatures as they had no need of sustenance as they were fed from solar power occasionally as they bedded down for the night, they did hear a fearsome bellowing which did make them a trite uneasy. However, whatever it was it seemed to have no interest in them. They rose early from the mossy bank that had been their overnight resting place and rose to their full stature. They rounded a bend and discovered that Alarm was waiting for them.

"I thought that I had better warn. you that you are being stalked by a fearsome creature and I have no idea what it is, you have probably heard it bellowing in the night," said the Alarm bird.

"Well, what does this? Terrifying creatures look like?" demanded a perplexed Atmos.

"You may not believe this, but it moves so fast that I haven't a clue what it looks like," said the Alarm bird.

"This is incredible, you are informing me that this animal moves so fast that you are unable to keep it in your vision, what a load of rubbish" Atmos retorted.

"You may not believe my interpretation of what I witnessed, and I fully understand your incredulity, but buthid is exactly what happened," said the alarmed bird.

The next instant Atmos's incredulity received a severe battering as a loud voice beseeched him not to tread on him. Atmos looked down at where his foot was about to tread and halted in mid-air, the reason being there was a diminutive being that was about to be crushed by his left foot.

"Thank you, a moment later you would have crushed me," said a voice.

Atmos looked down and immediately spotted the diminutive figure of a tiny being. Atmos was completely astounded as he stared at the minute being with the extremely loud voice.

"So, you do exist, and I accused. The alarm bird of it being a figment of his imagination. I owe him a great big apology," said Atmos.

"One of the reasons that I didn't believe him was he inferred that you moved incredibly fast at the speed of light," said Atmos.

"Do you mean like this?" said the minute being

"Like what? Was the instant response.

I am sorry but you missed it, I have been there and now I am back again.

By the way, my name is Tom, we have never been formally introduced" said the minute being

"This is getting stranger and stranger, It now appears that I have encountered a being that can travel faster than light, which is a terrific advantage if you have to get there in a hurry," said Atmos.

Bubbles, who had been watching the whole drama unfold was completely mesmerized by all the preceding.

"Well, it is partially a problem that I seemed to have created. I never realized that I would create a problem by traveling faster than light as you eloquently put it. What do you suggest that I do to remedy the matter?" Said Tom.

"Well, as you may imagine traveling at the speed of light is impossible to comprehend, as you may have arrived before you started your journey" continued Tom.

"Yes, but it must have considerable advantages when planning your journeys in the future although intricate timing has to be formulated," said Atmos.

"Do you mind if we stop talking about something which is essentially time travel, it's giving me a headache" moaned Bubbles.

They continued with their voyage of discovery without saying another word. Tom kept n disappearing and reappearing at frequent intervals., with all his manoeuvring it was impossible to gauge what speed they were achieving. However, it didn't really seem to matter as long as they got there eventually. As they breasted the brow of a hill and gazed at the sweeping meadows far below them, their vision locked on to a monstrous shape that lurked in the meadows. There was. In a blinding flash and Tom had disappeared and almost immediately re-appeared again.

"That is not a very nice creature, as soon as it spotted me, it attempted to incinerate me, it must be some kind of dragon, without any manners" reported Tom.

"Ok. Now we know what it is, how do we get rid of it? Questioned Tom.

"That should be easy enough chimed in the duopoly. We speak with one mind, and this gifts us with incredibly clear thinking," said the Duopoly.

"Ok, Tom the creature that tried to toast you. Was. Is it scaled and armoured questioned Atmos.

"Absolutely" he replied instantly.

"That is exactly the answer that I wanted to hear" retorted Atmos.

"Why did you find the answer was so correct," said Tom.

"Because we intend to slay this mythical beast" he replied.

"Then how exactly do you propose to accomplish that, this is a huge armoured plated monster that takes no prisoners," said Tom.

"This so-called dragon., Is a creature of heat and has an aversion to cold. We intend to freeze it and destroy it completely" replied Atmos.

Then having described his plan of action the duopoly took off flying in the direction of the monster. The creature was not to be taken by surprise and sent a great spume of fire in the direction of the duo. However, the flames seem to hit an invisible wall and could progress no further Except now it was the turn of the duopoly to play their hand. The invisible wall turned itself into a sheet of ice and the temperature fell dramatically. Then from nowhere, a wind of hurricane proportions smashed into the ice sheet, This had the effect of dropping the temperature even further and it plummeted downwards. The Duopoly then directed the freezing wind in the direction of the mythical beast that had been aimlessly spitting fire at the frozen wall, with little effect. It was then that the Duopoly went on the offensive and directed a howling wind down a corridor of ice. This transformed the complete interior into a blast freezer.

The freezing wind smashed into the armoured plated dragon with a searing intensity. Unfortunately, this mythical beast was far more adept at adjusting to a benign climate than the cold blast that smashed into him. Another unfortunate thing for the dragon was that it was sealed tight in the armored plate which compressed its body even further. The huge creature stood for a moment and then visibly shattered like a broken mirror.

"I wouldn't have believed that was possible if I hadn't witnessed it," said Tom.

"Many people have the same approach as you and have the approach that seeing is believing," said Atmos.

"Well, the wanderers have returned. I suppose I should congratulate you on a successful mission," said Tom.

"Yeah, I suppose our plan worked to perfection, the only thing that could have gone wrong would have been if we got roasted alive," said Bubbles.

"Well, I am still not certain how you managed to turn the tables on the dragon or even how you managed to blast freeze the creature but suffice it to say well done and bathe yourself in my admiration" replied Tom.

"Then, to be perfectly honest with you, we took a chance on the freezing aspect of the problem, and it came up trumps," said Bubbles.

"You are both trying to wriggle out excepting my admiration," said Tom.

"Yeah. we seem to be indulging ourselves in a great deal of physical adventure and luckily, we seem to be the victors. Luck is, however, a fickle lady, and offers only two options, winning or losing. Maybe it is time to quit the path to adventure while our luck holds out," said Atmos.

Bubbles unexpectedly interrupted saying

"We could of course adopt a different possibility and say we are at the beginning of an incredible streak of luck which could be never-ending Of course I may be totally wrong in which case I apologize in advance," he said.

"OK I follow your drift and I would like to have a chance to combat the fickleness of lady luck" replied Atmos.

"How do you intend to do that?" Queried Bubbles.

"By the simple process of tossing a coin and calling either heads or tails. I will give you the option of having the first call, If I win, we shall immediately curtail all expeditions," said Amos.

Bubbles thought for a moment. and cocked his head to one side and then said" I agree"

Amos then stepped back and paused for an instant before flipping the coin. Bubbles called heads it was tails. and all expeditions were cancelled immediately Isn't it amazing how civilizations come and go and yet can be decided by the toss of a coin?

In a galaxy a billion light years from a planet known as Earth, whose inhabitants ignored the constant warnings of their scientists on global warming. The inhabitants. of this planet known as Harmony lived full and exciting lives filled with joy and happiness.

ORIGINAL WORLDS BOOK TWO

AN IRISH GHOST STORY

Many years ago, when I was just a young lad, I went to stay on my uncle's farm in Ireland. After the Second World War and having defeated the Nazis who were inspired by Hitler, my uncle Major Hugh Harold, who had married his childhood sweetheart, my aunt Sheila who was the direct descendant of the great Irish patriot Daniel O'Connor.

The farm was situated in the village of Curracloe in the county of Wexford. The sole farmhand was Jim a ruddy-faced genial giant of a man who could only see the best in people. In the huge kitchen, there was an enormous Aga cooker which my aunt used to keep, warm the frequent tiny birds that had the misfortune to fall out of their nests. At the back of the farm, there was a sinister lake called Locana Beasties. This had a very dubious reputation as a young school child had drowned there. The whole lake was surrounded by gnarled old trees and you had the impression that you were constantly being spied upon.

My bedroom was situated over the main driveway that led to the house. One night I retired early to bed having been helping Jim, the farmhand with the milking. I still don't know why I went to, the window. But when I looked down through the window there was a huge black coach in the driveway below me. Then a frightening thing happened as the coach driver looked up and words entered my brain THERE IS ROOM FOR ONE MORE

The next day I informed my uncle about what had happened he then old me that the coach of Gomorra, who was sometimes known as the death coach.

Anyway, I didn't think any more of the comment until over twenty years later when I had a job in the city selling specialized products. I had just entered. A vast building called Plantation House to see a client on the fourteenth floor and made a successful sale. I then pressed the button to summon the lift. my return journey. The lift arrived but this time there was a lift attendant whose eyes transfixed me, and a voice bored into my brain There IS ROOM FOR ONE MORE. I instantly leaped back, and the lift went hurtled down killing all twenty-two of its occupants, you may ask me if there is a moral to this story. This must be taken as good advice, specifically if the advisor is the harbinger of death.

THE SNEEZE

It crept up behind you like a sneaky smell and invited you in to linger and dwell.
It invades your thoughts and subconscious mind to enable it to make you blind.
Why should I do this I hear you ask, because you must be ready to fulfill its dreadful task.
Its insidious movement is meant to distract from the ghastly thing that it will enact.
As it gets nearer it will try to ease, the horror of a gigantic sneeze.
It is arriving now and moving fast, the sneeze has arrived with a tremendous blast.
What happened next is for you to suggest but it has blown off my head, my legs and my chest.

HAPPINESS

You may be content but that is not happy.
You suffer from anger and are incredibly snappy.
Being content is being quite lazy, sure things will happen, but they are still quite hazy.
What you need is excitement and adventure.
You have the right mind far and wide you will venture.
Happiness is a glorious state of mind, sadness and grief are left far behind.
Throw off your troubles and get rid of your clothes, frolic in the sand let it seep through your toes.
Happiness is the true wonder of life; children are born to the husband and life.
Do you need riches? And a super fast car, not really you say, perhaps a drink at the bar?
So how do you define what is happy or fake?
Not as easy as I thought, content was the same, I made a mistake.

SINISTER

There is someone behind you, what do you do? speed up you're walking or hide in the loo.

It's a terrible night and it's started to rain; how do I hide from the anguish and pain?

A creature emerges on the path just ahead, it's missing a face, and I think it is dead.

It staggers towards me with an ungainly gate, and no time to avoid it, what is my fate?

It lurches towards me its mouth is agape, and I think I may scream and then I wake up it was only a dream.

HIS RAGE

His desire WAS INTENSE FOR FAME POWER AND GLORY.
HE SIMMERED WITH ANGER AND HIS FEATURES BECAME RED.
HE SHOUTED AND SCREAMED I WISH I WERE DEAD.
 IT BUBBLED UP INSIDE HIM, AN INTENSE Uncontrollable Rage.
What have I ACHIEVED IN MY LONG WASTEFUL life? THE WARS CONTINUE REDEMPTION P AND DOWN AND EXPLODED WITH FURY.
 THE ULTIMATE PRIZE, WHICH IS ONLY OBTAINED BY THE GOOD AND THE wise AROUND ME AND TROUBLE AND STRIFE.
I SEACH FOR

ER AND TRAPPED IN A CAGE.
HE PACED U

Printed in Great Britain
by Amazon